YESTERDAY'S LOVE SONG

YESTERDAY'S LOVE SONG

•

JAN McDANIEL

AVALON BOOKS
THOMAS BOUREGY AND COMPANY, INC.
401 LAFAYETTE STREET
NEW YORK, NEW YORK 10003

Library of Congress Catalog Card Number: 94-94016
ISBN 0-8034-9044-5

PRINTED IN THE UNITED STATES OF AMERICA
ON ACID-FREE PAPER
BY HADDON CRAFTSMEN, SCRANTON, PENNSYLVANIA

To Beth,
a good friend

Chapter One

A misty rain had begun to fall, dulling the landscape with a silver sheen. Tracy quickened her stride over the once familiar terrain, partially blinded by the raindrops that dotted her glasses. It mattered little—her vision was already streaked by tears she'd been holding back all morning and could keep in no longer.

The rain beaded in her short blond hair, making it curl tight as springs, but she never considered turning back. Her tears were a private weakness, one she didn't want anyone to see.

Stomping through ankle-high weeds, she reached the edge of the woods, scanning the field for familiar landmarks. She felt for a moment as if it had been another lifetime when she'd come here almost daily seeking solitude from the madness of everyday life.

She bit her lip so hard it hurt. Her hands at her sides knotted into fists.

Shannon was dead, and things were never going to be the same again.

They'd come here together sometimes—on happier days just to fish and laugh, on darker ones to hash out their problems.

But that was back in high school, and life had been so simple then. This wasn't the future she'd imagined.

Confused about which way to go, she stopped and closed her eyes. At twenty-seven, she was the girl from Cherry Cove, Texas, who had her own television show and what everyone termed a promising career ahead of her. It was just an afternoon talk show on a Dallas station, but she'd already had some contact with the networks and was sure the offer she dreamed about would be coming.

How little her hard work and small victories seemed to mean now that she'd come back to her hometown to bury one of her best friends. A friend she'd lost touch with over the years because of her own preoccupation with her career.

Guilt flooded through her as she spotted the overgrown path and proceeded down it. Was all the scrambling worth it when it drew her away from things and people she loved?

Shannon had wanted her to stay here. But she couldn't, and she'd set off seeking the glamorous life her heart had imagined. She kicked at a clump of wet weeds.

Less than a week ago her life had seemed to be in such perfect order. Now, she questioned everything about it.

Navigating the incline, she reached the narrow creek bank. Her eyes widened, and a slight comfort settled over her heart as she surveyed the familiar surroundings. This was one place the years hadn't changed.

The narrow, crooked creek trickled by, bubbling with raindrops. She remembered how cool the water used to feel when they'd waded in it on scorching summer afternoons.

She sighed deeply, removing her glasses and rubbing at the free-flowing tears on her cheeks with a fist.

The air smelled damp and tangy. She inhaled it.

Gazing at the bank, she could almost see Shannon sitting there in cutoffs and a T-shirt, holding a fishing pole over the water, smiling that devilish grin of his and pushing back the shock of blond hair that always bobbed over his forehead, his bare feet dangling into the water.

The unexpected rustling of leaves startled her.

She turned quickly, jerking her head up to face a tall, slim figure she thought at first was a mirage.

Fumbling with the glasses in her hand, she hurriedly put them back on.

The intruder's startled expression reflected her own, then melted into one of his rare but striking smiles. ''Hi, Hotshot,'' he said quietly.

She wasn't sure if it was the sight of Rick that got to her or the sound of the long-forgotten nickname. He and Shannon had always called her Hotshot because she had such big and seemingly impossible dreams.

''Hi, yourself, Cowboy,'' she choked back through a flood of uncontrollable tears. ''I didn't know you were in town.''

''I missed the funeral this morning. I wasn't going to come. Then I realized at the last minute I had to.''

His charcoal-gray eyes looked damp, and Tracy didn't think it was entirely from the rain.

''I guess it's just the two of us now,'' she said, gazing into the creek bed.

Rick moved closer. ''I'm having a hard time believing this. Shannon was the one who wanted to stay here where it was quiet and settled and safe. Then he gets himself killed in a car wreck.''

An overwhelming grief welled up inside her, and Tracy covered her face in her hands, attempting to mask a sob.

A protective instinct took over, and Rick stepped in front of her, folding her into his arms. She fell easily against his chest without shyness, burying her head in his T-shirt.

He held her firmly, images tumbling through his mind of how often in the old days he'd wished he could hold her like this. But he'd never dared. Tracy had always been wild about Shannon. Rick had been the third wheel.

Now, after all these years, she was in his arms seeking comfort for her loss.

Guilt prodded him. Shannon had been his friend, too. He shouldn't be jealous of someone whose life had been cut short.

"Go ahead and cry, Trace," he urged. "There's no one here but us and the chipmunks."

And he had seen her cry before. All the times when Shannon had let her down. He'd wanted to tell her so many times she was hung up on the wrong guy, but he hadn't wanted to gamble with her friendship or Shannon's.

She felt small and warm in his arms. Without realizing it, he tightened his hold on her.

Could it be that after all these years he'd never stopped caring about her? he wondered suddenly.

Knowing he would see her here had been what nearly kept him away from his best friend's funeral.

Was it fate that he'd come down to the creek to be alone and run smack into her? Or was it just some cruel joke of circumstances?

He should go, he thought, hightail it back to Houston. But he couldn't just leave her here. He threaded his fingers through the satiny mass of curls on her head. She smelled of oranges and jasmine. The sophisticated, unfamiliar yet intriguing fragrance reminded him everything had changed. Tracy was part of another world now—so was he.

Tracy allowed herself to lean against Rick, drawing from his strength. He'd always been as quiet as Shannon was outgoing. He was as steady and strong and stable as Shannon had been unpredictable.

His T-shirt smelled of fabric softener, and she detected the scent of soap beneath it. Despite his lanky frame, the muscles of his chest were hard.

Her tears spent, Tracy found herself reluctant to draw herself out of his steadying arms. It had been a long time since she'd had anywhere to run to.

She listened to the patter of raindrops hitting the leaves, the gurgle of the creek, the beating of Rick's heart.

Finally, she pulled back, suddenly embarrassed and knowing she must look awful from crying.

"I'm sorry," she said, looking up at him as though seeing him for the first time. He still had the same even features, the black hair with just a hint of a wave in it. But there was maturity mingled with the boyishness she recalled.

"Don't be," he countered, not releasing her.

"You've grown a mustache," she said, forcing a

smile on her tear-streaked face, raising a finger to trace the band over his lip.

A shock wave rippled through Rick at her touch. He fought back an overwhelming urge to kiss her. This was just like Tracy. She didn't realize what she did to people.

Tracy watched his eyes change and impulsively wanted to stand on tiptoe and kiss him. Out of gratitude for being here for her, she reasoned.

But something kept her from acting out her impulse.

Why did kissing an old friend seem so out of line?

Abruptly, he released her, stepping back.

He was getting all caught up in it again, he thought. All caught up in her, and that was the last thing he wanted.

Rick answered her questioning expression with a long, low look. Life had always been easy for people like Tracy and Shannon. Not for him.

"I can't be Shannon for you," he said.

Tracy's head snapped up as though she'd been slapped.

Her lips parted in indignant denial, but she couldn't find the words to protest.

And part of her own mind echoed his accusation. The three of them had always been together. She associated Shannon and Rick so closely. Had she been thinking of Shannon while she cried in Rick's arms, imagining he was still there for her? While she didn't want to believe that, she couldn't swear it wasn't true.

A polished fingernail flew to her lips. The whole world had turned upside down today. And in some unintentional way, she'd hurt a good friend.

"I'm sorry, Rick," she sputtered, raking a hand through her hair. She stepped back as though Satan himself were standing there. "It's a difficult time for both of us."

Guilt stabbed at him as he watched the conflicting emotions cross her reddened but still pretty face. He'd sought to comfort her and ended up making her more upset. Why did he have to lash out at her? She couldn't help it that he'd always been in love with her. She didn't even know it.

He stepped forward.

"Trace, wait . . . " he said.

"I've got to go," she said, inching away.

Finally, she broke into a run, ignoring his pleas for her to stay.

The soles of her tennis shoes squashed against the wet leaves on the ground, and she tripped over a fern and nearly slid down the incline. But she managed to scramble up.

And on the way, she tried to drive from her mind the odd feeling she'd experienced in his arms. What it was, she didn't know, and right now she was too confused to sort it out.

* * *

Tracy sat in the sprawling dining room of the Victorian house her parents had turned into a bed-and-breakfast, one leg tucked under the other in the carved maple chair as she picked up a silver fork and attacked it with the polishing cloth.

Her mother walked into the room and studied her daughter, who was showing the fork no mercy.

"You don't have to do that, Tracy," she insisted.

Late-afternoon sunlight streamed in through the lace curtains, casting broken patterns on the walls and Mrs. Madison's antique furniture.

Tracy didn't miss a stroke as she answered her mother. "I don't mind. I need something to do."

"You're on vacation."

Tracy nodded in acknowledgement but didn't pause.

"You said yourself the silverware was badly in need of polishing."

Alice Madison placed her hands on her slight hips and stared futilely at her daughter. The sunbeams played on the silver streaks in the older woman's hair. She and her husband had had their only child late in life, before midlife babies had become fashionable.

Now she looked on helplessly, knowing her daughter was in pain and unsure what to do about it.

"Vacations are for resting, relaxing."

Tracy had agreed to take the two weeks off while

she was home for Shannon's funeral only because Hank, her producer, had insisted. She wasn't sure now that it was a good idea. Here, she was surrounded by so many memories. In Dallas, she'd have her work to concentrate on.

The doorbell rang. She and her mother exchanged glances.

"I'll get it," Tracy offered.

Alice motioned for her to stay put. "I'm already up," she indicated, already halfway to the door.

Tracy heard the wooden door swing open, followed by her mother's voice. "Rick! How good to see you!"

Rick. Even though Tracy couldn't see them, she knew her mother was giving him a bear hug.

Tracy set the silverware down on the table. She colored at the memory of the scene in the woods earlier. Why had Rick come here? It was good that he had, she thought, rising from her chair. While he'd been there to console her this morning, she'd been too wrapped up in her own loss to comfort him. Once again, she'd failed a friend.

Listening to the sound of her mother's voice approaching, she met them in the archway between the living room and dining room.

"Rick's here, Tracy," her mother announced, as though she'd found a stray puppy in the woods.

Tracy faced him, looking up into silver-gray eyes.

"Hello, Rick," she said evenly. "I'm glad you came over."

Her impulse was to hug him as her mother had, but remembering he was mad at her, she held back.

Rick gazed around the dining room, feeling as though time had stood still. The massive maple table, the crocheted placemats, the lingering scent of furniture polish—everything was just as he remembered it ten years ago. Even Tracy, for all her success, was still wearing three-dollar tennis shoes.

"Can I get you something to eat?" Alice offered. "We've got some lemon meringue pie."

"No, thank you, Mrs. Madison," he declined. "I just came to talk to Tracy."

The older woman nodded approvingly.

"Let's go for a walk," Tracy suggested quickly.

Rick nodded in silent agreement.

"Maybe you'll want some pie when you get back," Mrs. Madison suggested.

Tracy led the way to the front door, proceeding outside and waiting for Rick to follow. She stood on the wide front porch that wrapped around two sides of the yellow and beige frame house, sporting wooden rockers, hanging plants, and a swing.

The sun had dried all traces of this morning's rain, leaving the June air hot and muggy. Tracy wished she had changed her jeans for shorts.

When Rick closed the door and reached her, she didn't start walking immediately.

"Look, I'm sorry about this morning," she volunteered. "You're the last person on earth I want to fight with right now."

Looking down on her, Rick felt a tightening in his chest. After all these years apart, he still harbored that old tender, protective feeling toward her. He didn't want to squabble with her, either—yet he almost felt he had to in self-defense.

The sunlight gave her hair a golden sheen, haloing wide, sparkling blue eyes fringed with long dark lashes behind the oval frames of her glasses. Her face was rounded with a small, almost pouty mouth that stayed a deep cherry color without benefit of lipstick.

No wonder television viewers were captivated by her. No wonder Shannon had been. No wonder he still was.

He had no doubt she'd reach the big networks one day. She had the looks, the bubbly personality, and, most of all, the gumption.

But under it all was the fragile young woman who had cried in his arms this morning. He knew her, he supposed, better than anybody. Back in the old days, she'd shared confidences with him she wouldn't have with Shannon. Rick had always been safe to her because she wasn't in love with him.

He had no right to have ever fallen in love with her. But that was a long time ago.

"It was my fault," he said. "I overreacted. Shannon's death has been a strain on all of us."

Tracy, relieved to have his forgiveness for whatever she had done, flashed him a bright smile.

"I don't think you and I have ever had an argument before," she observed.

He shrugged. Their relationship had always been quiet, unmarred by the storms she and Shannon experienced. But it had lacked the passion as well.

"Come on, let's walk," she coaxed. "I'm getting restless sitting around here."

He took long, easy strides as he set off down the gravel, curling road. She matched him two for one to keep up.

"It's quieter here than in the city," he noted idly. "A nice change."

"A little too quiet," she countered. "All I ever used to think about was getting away."

"You seemed to have managed that fine."

She sighed deeply. "I get homesick sometimes for this place."

"Me, too."

"How's your family?"

"Great. My sister, Gina, got married last year."

"What about your little brother, Billy?"

"He graduated from high school this year. He's still obnoxious, but one of the smartest kids I've ever seen."

"I remember when ya'll moved away. I cried for

days." Rick's father had lost his job at a factory in a neighboring town a few months before she and Rick and Shannon were to graduate, and the Evans family had been forced to move to Houston.

"It turned out all right, I suppose."

"I always imagined the three of us would just go right on being friends."

"I guess we did, even though we weren't together. You always knew you were going to leave."

She glanced sidewise at him. "What are you doing now?" she asked.

He shrugged. "Construction work. It's a living."

She nodded. That explained all those muscles.

"Still riding in the rodeos?"

A smile rose to his lips. "On weekends sometimes. When I can make the time to get away."

"So are you married? Engaged?"

He gave her an amused smile. "No." Impossible. He'd compared everyone he'd dated to her, and no one had ever measured up. "What about you?"

"Too busy."

"Too busy or too hung up on Shannon still?"

He knew he was treading on a mine field by bringing it up, but he had to know.

"That was over a long time ago. I hadn't even seen him since right after I graduated from college."

"This is me you're talking to. I'm the one you'd come to whenever he got into one of his moods and things blew up between the two of you. You said once Shannon was the only person you'd ever marry.''

''You have a long and harsh memory. That was a seventeen-year-old girl talking. He never forgave me for leaving.''

''Don't believe that. He knew you had to go. We both did.''

''I guess, in a way, I never stopped loving him. A part of me always will.''

Her admission washed through Rick like a bucket of ice water. Well, it was what he had expected, wasn't it?

She stopped abruptly, turning to face him. ''I'm glad you came, Rick. You've always been the one person I could really talk to about anything.''

An odd expression she couldn't define crossed his face.

''That's pretty rare, isn't it?'' he asked, wondering what would happen if he dared tell her how he'd been feeling all these years.

''Precious.'' She identified it with a smile. ''Let's stay in touch, okay? It's a short flight from Dallas to Houston.''

His expression grew hard as the Texas soil. ''Maybe it's best to just leave things as they are. We both might have good intentions right now, but when we get back to our normal lives, we'll forget all about them.''

She'd never understand how hard it was for him to see her, he thought.

His rebuff disappointed her. Seeing him again evoked such warm feelings inside her, and now she was going to have to turn her back on those. The life she'd chosen was not without sacrifices. Still, she didn't see why they couldn't arrange to meet from time to time, why he was so opposed to even trying.

"How long are you staying in town?" she asked.

He shrugged evasively. "Not long." He'd thought seeing her might prove he was finally over her. But it wasn't working. All the old feelings were stronger than ever. Best to get away while he still had his pride.

Tracy resumed her walking. Rick was acting strange, she reflected. Well, people change over the years, and she knew Shannon's death was devastating to him as well.

They'd passed through the town's small residential district and were smack downtown, in a scant two-block area of old brick buildings that housed a post office, fire station, bank, and a few shops. Main Street was the only one in town that didn't twist and turn.

"Look," she said, pointing across the street to the two-story furniture store. "That's Shannon's store."

A wreath hung over the door just above the Closed sign.

Rick offered a sad smile. "He accomplished what he said he would. He said he would build this town into something. I understand people drive in from Houston to shop here."

"Mom says he has a lot of unusual antique reproductions. People thought he was crazy when he first opened it, but it brings in a lot of people and benefits the whole town. I wonder what will happen to the store now."

"I guess his grandmother will take it over."

"Cilla's pretty old. This is really hard on her. Let's go see her, Rick. I've been worried about her all day. Seeing you might make her feel better."

He nodded. "I was planning to see her before I left town."

"It's not far," she said, already heading toward Poplar Street.

Shannon's grandmother lived in a modest white frame house tucked back from the road in a dense cluster of trees. The front yard resembled a small park, with its well-tended flower beds, concrete birdbath, and latticework arbor.

Several cars were still parked around the side of the house, and Tracy realized people were still here from this morning's funeral. She hesitated as she grew conscious of her casual attire—jeans, a T-shirt and tennis shoes.

"What's wrong?" Rick asked.

"I'm really not dressed for visiting," she said.

"You look fine. You know Cilla would be glad to see you even in rags."

Before she could decide one way or another, the front door flew open, and a permed head popped out. Tracy recognized Shannon's Aunt Patsy from Midland, whom she'd met this morning.

"Come on in, Tracy," the woman called.

Tracy approached the small porch, introducing Rick to Shannon's aunt as she walked.

Patsy ushered them inside. The bright little house looked unusually dark. Shannon's grandmother was sitting in a rocker beside the piano, her frame even frailer than usual, her normally bright blue eyes as colorless as her white hair.

"I brought Rick," Tracy said simply, hating how much she sounded like her mother had earlier.

The woman's eyes flickered, and she rose with great effort to give Rick a hug. "I'm so glad you've come," she said, her voice rippling with emotion.

As a threatening lump rose in her throat, Tracy looked away.

Finally, Rick sat down beside the old woman. Tracy dropped down on the sofa across the room. She fiddled with the doily draped across its arm, listening as Rick and Cilla talked softly, watching the calming effect he had on her.

That was Rick, always a rock when the whole world was falling apart. Over the years, she'd thought frequently of Shannon and how much she missed him. Now she realized it hadn't been only Shannon she'd missed.

Patsy, who had disappeared into the kitchen, emerged to bring her a slice of chocolate cake and a cup of coffee she didn't want.

Although her stomach turned at the sight of the food, Tracy thanked her and set it on the end table. She noticed Rick did the same with his.

Across the room, Cilla threw her thin hands in the air. "I just don't know what to do about the store. I don't have the heart to do anything about it right now."

Patsy gave her a stern look. "Now, Mom, I told you Sam was coming to take care of it for you."

Cilla hooted. "In a week. He takes his sweet time."

From her tone, Tracy guessed Cilla wasn't much impressed with the prospect of Sam, whoever he was, coming at all.

"He has business to wrap up in Midland," Patsy reported impatiently. She glanced at Rick and Tracy. "Sam's my son," she explained.

"Shannon left him the store?" Tracy asked. She'd assumed Shannon would have left it to Cilla—he'd always diligently taken care of her. If a twenty-eight-year-old thought to make a will at all—she'd never considered needing one.

''We think he must have,'' Cilla explained, ''although it will be another week before we know for sure. You see, I own half of the business. Shannon insisted on that. He said if anything ever happened to him, he'd make sure I had a partner who was young enough and strong enough to run it. At the time I thought he was talking nonsense—'' Her voice broke.

Tracy leaned forward. ''I can keep it open until Sam arrives.''

All eyes turned to her.

''That's very kind of you, dear,'' Cilla said. ''But you've got your television show.''

''And two weeks' vacation with little to do,'' she said. ''Please let me do this for you, Cilla.''

''I'll help her,'' Rick assured Cilla.

Tracy's eyes flared in quiet astonishment, flying to Rick. He'd told her he was leaving soon.

His eyes squared on her. ''You might be able to sell furniture, but you can't lift it by yourself.''

Tracy conceded he was right. Besides, she was grateful for his help. She knew nothing of running a store.

Cilla appraised the two young people in her living room. Shannon had been telling her for years he'd believed his two best friends felt more than friendship for each other. Until now, she'd never believed it.

She gave them a thin smile in acceptance of their generous offer and didn't mention the store had employees who were quite capable of lifting furniture.

Chapter Two

As they walked silently back through the downtown area in the direction of Tracy's parents' house, Tracy stared at the furniture store across the street. The ring of keys Cilla had pressed into her hand just a few minutes ago jangled in the pocket of her jeans.

Tomorrow morning she'd be opening that store and trying to figure out what to do. Clearly, she'd ventured out of her realm. But in her desperation to help Cilla, she'd been willing to volunteer maybe just a tad too quickly.

"This is a fine mess you've gotten us into." Rick's voice cut through the silence as though he'd been reading her thoughts.

Tracy giggled. Quickly, she cut her laughter short.

"It's okay to laugh," Rick urged. "Life goes on, you know."

"I suppose Shannon would have wanted it that way," she philosophized. "He never hesitated to crack a joke, anytime, anywhere."

"Maybe that's why he could make people feel so good when he was around."

Tracy nodded, pushing her glasses up on the bridge of her nose. "I suppose I have gotten us into a mess. But I'd like to remind you I didn't have you in a halfnelson when you chimed in with your offer."

"Maybe I feel as guilty as you do about not having stayed in touch with Shannon."

Her face flushed crimson. "I'm not doing this out of guilt," she insisted, not sure herself her words were true. "I just want to help Cilla out. Anyway, I'm glad I won't be doing this alone."

Rick glanced down at her. He wondered if his hasty gesture had had anything to do with Shannon at all, or was he too much of a coward to pass up a chance to spend time with her?

"I'm not sure how much help I'll be. The furniture business is as far out of my line as it is yours."

She smiled up at him, and his chest constricted. She was even prettier now than she'd been years ago.

"We'll manage," she insisted with blind assurance.

"Sure we will," he echoed. "I just hope Sam

shows up pretty quick. Shannon never mentioned his cousin."

"He probably never saw a need to if the cousin lives in Midland. I wonder if he's at all like Shannon was."

"No one is like Shannon was," Rick noted dryly.

A thoughtful expression crossed Tracy's face. "I thought you had to get back to Houston. You won't be in trouble with your job, will you?"

"No. I'll just make a few phone calls tonight. I have some time off coming."

He didn't understand why he didn't tell her it was his company and he could take off when he pleased. But if he did, he would have had to explain why he'd told her earlier he couldn't stay.

"Where are you staying?" she asked.

"I was going to drive back tonight. I guess I'll get a room over in Two Forks."

"Don't be silly. Why drive all that way when you can stay at the best and only bed-and-breakfast in town for free?"

Rick had known the offer was coming. He hesitated. Working with her all day was going to be hard enough. Staying in the same house with her, how long was it going to be before he blurted his real feelings and shattered their friendship forever? He'd just lost one friend—he didn't want to lose another.

Tracy puzzled over his reluctance.

"I don't want to put your parents to any bother," he insisted.

"It's their business. They won't mind."

"Then they'll have to let me pay for the room."

"You can bicker over that with them. Just say you'll stay."

"All right," he agreed with all the enthusiasm of a man bound for the gallows.

Tracy reached out and squeezed his hand. His palm felt tough, but smoother than she expected. "It will be kind of like old times again," she said.

Rick shook his head, aching inside as he looked down into her sparkling eyes. "No," he insisted sadly. "The old times are gone, Hotshot."

Blinking rapidly, she looked away and released his hand. For the second time today, she felt she'd offended him and didn't understand how.

At her reaction, Rick wanted to kick himself. Maybe everything would be easier if he came clean and told her the truth. But he couldn't, not now, not while she was trying to cope with Shannon's death.

He wrapped an arm around her shoulder. "Don't be mad," he said. "You know you can't ever go back. And if you think about it, would you really want to?"

Tracy eyed him skeptically. "You've changed, Rick," she proclaimed.

Rick considered. He had. After moving away, breaking free of Shannon's shadow, he'd found his own strengths and potential. He doubted if he would have been anywhere near as successful had he stayed here where everyone thought of him right off as Shannon's friend instead of seeing him for who he was.

"The years do that," he agreed. "I think you've changed more than you know."

Tracy sighed, catching the aroma of dinner cooking from the town's single diner. She realized she hadn't eaten all day.

"I'm hungry," she said. "How about you?"

Rick nodded. "You want to stop?"

She shook her head. "I left my purse back at the house."

"I've got some money."

"I really don't feel like being around a lot of people. I can fix something back at the house."

He raised a dark eyebrow. "You've learned to cook?"

"I fry a mean hamburger," she countered.

"A hamburger sounds good," he agreed. He looked up at the sky. "But we'd better hurry. I think it's going to rain again."

"You're right," she said, speeding up.

Rick watched her ease ahead of him. No matter what he accomplished in life, he reflected, something would always be missing until his feelings for Tracy were resolved, one way or the other. And for the sake of his own sanity, before this week was out, he was going to set everything straight.

Tracy stood on the back porch, her arms folded across her chest as she leaned against a pillar. A few feet down, Rick sat propped on the porch railing.

The night was silent except for a chorus of crickets and the rustling of leaves in the breeze. The threatening rain hadn't materialized into anything more than a drizzle, and it had stopped now.

"You do make a decent hamburger," Rick told her approvingly.

"Only because I was hungry. If I wasn't, they'd turn out lousy."

"That's your secret?" he asked, rising. He stretched his lean frame, too restless to sit still.

"It's been a long day, hasn't it?" she asked.

"A very long day," he agreed. "I think I'll go for a walk. I feel tired, but not to sleep."

"Do you mind if I tag along?" she asked.

He gave her a long, low look. "Why would I mind?"

"I thought you might want to be alone."

His lips curved into a half-smile. "Come on."

"I don't know if I could sleep, either," she said as she descended the steps. "Not that I normally have a problem with insomnia. I'm usually exhausted by the time my head hits the pillow."

"Me, too," he said, heading off across the moonlit field. "Unless I have something on my mind."

Tracy fell silent for a moment, staying in step beside him.

"Pretty night," she ventured, tossing back her headful of curls.

Rick tried not to look at her, but he couldn't help himself. Her hair was a halo, her cheeks flushed from the brisk walk. He slowed his gait. It was ridiculous to think he could run from her.

"Fog's setting in," he noted.

"It looks eerie, like we're on some remote planet." She shivered involuntarily.

"Are you cold?" he asked.

She shook her head. "No. It's not at all cool out here."

Suddenly he startled her by reaching out and lifting her hand from her side. He stopped walking, closely examining her fingers.

"What are you doing?" she asked, disquieted by his scrutiny and the strange prickling feeling his unexpected touch produced—like a thousand hot needles stabbing the length of her arm.

"When did you start wearing nail polish?" he asked.

"It looks good on camera. Don't you like it?"

"It's just something different. You never used to wear it."

Tracy's brows drew together. "I guess I was too

busy being a tomboy. Rick, if I could wish for one person in the world to be here with me right now, it would be you. I almost can't believe you're here. But it's so funny. In some ways I feel we're strangers.''

He stood close beside her, his eyes intent upon her. She'd always liked his eyes, she reflected. They held an unflinching warmth and honesty and kindness. That hadn't changed. No matter what the world dished out, she'd always found solace in those eyes.

''We'll never be strangers,'' he said. ''But maybe we never knew each other as well as we thought we did.''

''But something is different,'' she said. She couldn't describe it, but she felt almost awkward in his presence tonight. Tense.

His gaze strayed off across the field. ''Maybe because it's just the two of us, without Shannon to divert our attention.''

Fresh grief welled up inside her. ''Maybe it's just that I feel strange. I suppose I've led a sheltered life. I haven't had to cope with death before.''

His voice was as steady and gentle as the breeze. ''I know it's hard. There's nothing I can do to make it easier for you.''

''You have. By being here. How about you?''

''It seems unreal to me. I suppose because I haven't seen him for so long. I get angry, and I wonder why it was Shannon. When something like this happens, you ask yourself a lot of tough questions."

The set of her jaw hardened. "I've been asking myself some lately."

She crossed her arms and stared at the full moon. "Like whether what I'm going after is what I really want."

"You've wanted your television career since back in junior high school."

"Yeah, well last week I would have told you I was happy as a clam. Now I'm not so sure. I mean, look at my parents. They have what a lot of people would consider a dull life, and are they unhappy?"

"They run their own business and meet new people constantly. Besides, they're not you. And you're not them. You're the craziest person I ever met, Tracy Madison. You've spent ten years chasing a brass ring, and now that it's in reach, you're going to pull back and let it slip away."

Her hands flew to her slender hips. "I am not crazy, Rick Evans! My whole life is passing me by in a blur. Maybe I want time for other things besides work."

"What things?"

"I don't know."

"You're not going to move back here?" he asked in horror.

"I might," she confessed.

He shook his head. "I guess I did have you figured wrong. I never took you for a quitter."

She tilted her chin. "I guess I had you pegged wrong, too. I thought you were the one person that didn't matter to. I always thought it was enough with you that I could just be myself."

His voice softened. "It is, Hotshot. You know that. Just don't get scared and back off now that you're so close. You don't want to have to live with that. People talk about you, you know, even in Houston. You are famous."

"I'm not famous."

"You've got people loving to watch you. You've got to follow through with it."

She dropped her hands to her side. "I am tired," she admitted.

"Come on," he said, resisting a longing to bundle her into his arms. "Let's go back. Everything will be clearer in the morning."

She laughed, then let out a yelp. "In the morning I'm going to be up to my neck in furniture I don't know what to do with."

"*We* are going to be up to our necks in furniture," he corrected. "You can wing it. Just—what do they say?—ad-lib."

"Yeah." They reached the door of the house and stepped onto the porch. Tracy opened the sliding-glass door that led into the rec room, the one room of the house off-limits to guests.

While the other rooms looked like they belonged in another era, this one was totally 90s. A stereo and television centered one wall while the others teemed with cinder block and wood shelves that held books and board games. A long sofa with soft, bulging cushions faced the television, and beanbag chairs were scattered on the floor. A pool table filled the opposite side of the room.

Sliding the door shut and snapping the lock, she looked up at him. "Good night, Rick," she said.

"Good night," he replied.

She turned away, then turned back and caught hold of his forearm, standing on tiptoe to grace his cheek with a kiss.

His skin was rough and hot, and he smelled of night air and pine. She had intended the kiss to be casual, but as she brushed against him, something powerful coursed through her.

As she drew back, her eyes met his, and she saw something there she couldn't decipher.

"Good night," she repeated, backing away.

Only when she was racing upstairs did he raise the back of his hand to touch the spot on his face that still tingled as though it had been brushed by the wing of a bird.

Sooner or later, he realized, he was going to have to tell her the truth.

* * *

Early the next morning, Rick wandered into the kitchen and found Alice Madison bustling over the stove, humming as she worked. A faint smile rose to his lips as he watched her.

Finally, she paused, wiping the back of one hand across her brow and spying him hovering in the hallway.

"Good morning, Rick," she greeted him, automatically reaching into a cupboard for a mug.

By the time he entered the room, she had poured it full of steaming coffee and was holding it out to him.

Gratefully, he accepted it. "Thanks," he said.

"Sit down," she offered, with a sweeping gesture toward a small white painted wooden table pushed off to one corner of the immense, sparkling kitchen. She looked thoughtful. "Unless you'd like to go in the dining room with the other guests? We're having quiche and orange-pecan muffins this morning."

Rick grimaced. "Thanks, but I think I'll hold out for bacon and eggs at the diner," he said.

No sooner had he said it than she was sliding a frying pan out of a cabinet. "If you want bacon and eggs, you'll get them right here," she declared.

"I don't want to be any bother," he insisted, reluctantly sliding into a chair.

She dismissed him with an expansive wave. "It's been a long time since I had you boys here to cook for." She caught herself and paused. "Shannon never came by much after Tracy left. And you should be horsewhipped for not coming by. Houston's only a few hours away."

He sipped the hot, rich coffee. "It's hard to come back."

She nodded over the sizzling frying pan. "It wasn't me either of you came to see, anyway," she said slyly. "Tracy was the attraction here."

Rick studied the inside of the coffee cup. "You know she's talking about staying here."

Alice nodded. "A fool idea if I ever heard one. I hope you can talk her out of it. She always listened to you."

"Doesn't seem to want to now," he noted.

She presented him with a plate of bacon and eggs, went back to the counter for her own mug of coffee, then sat beside him at the table.

"She's neglected a part of her life that's catching up to her now is what it is," she speculated. "Her sights have been set so long on this television thing, she never had time for a home and family. She doesn't realize it, but she's missing that now."

Rick wondered if Mrs. Madison's observation couldn't apply as easily to him. Except he knew he missed having a family and a home. He pushed himself into his work to fill that emptiness.

A buzzer sounded, and Mrs. Madison rose. "The problem is, she's just too fickle. No one is ever right for her."

She moved to the counter in search of an oven mitt. "The guests will be up shortly."

Tracy appeared in the hallway, dressed primly in a blue linen suit, pumps, and a starchy white blouse with a high collar fringed with the slightest touch of lace.

Her sleepy eyes widened when she spotted Rick at the table.

"Good morning." She addressed both him and her mother.

"Good morning," her mother replied. "Do you want breakfast?"

She shook her head, bound for the cupboard where she secured a mug. "Just coffee, thanks."

Rick watched as she poured it.

"I think I'll take this out on the back porch," she announced after adding generous amounts of milk and sugar. She looked inquiringly at Rick. "Do you want to bring yours?"

He took the mug and followed her outside.

She sat on the railing, sipping the coffee and watching him as he planted himself on a step.

"How did you sleep last night?"

"Fine," he lied. "The room's nice and quiet. A little frillier than what I'm used to."

She laughed lightly. "I suppose it would be. Mom gets carried away with her decorating."

"How did you sleep?" he asked.

"Fine," she lied. "It always takes me a while to

get going in the morning." She'd tossed and turned, reliving the old days in her mind, reexamining events long over. As hard as she tried, she'd been unable to purge her mind of the thought of Rick's presence in the house, the burning sensation his cheek had left on her lips when she'd kissed his face last night.

If she didn't know better, if it had been anyone else, she would have concluded she was attracted to him. But this was Rick. Her pal, her buddy, her confidant from years gone by. Her reaction to him now was absurd.

She chalked it up to her present state of mind. She wondered what Rick would think if he knew she was having feelings about him that had nothing to do with friendship. He'd probably get a good laugh out of it.

Maybe that was the best tact. Just get it out in the open so they could share the joke. Ten years ago that's exactly what she would have done. But for a reason she couldn't understand, she didn't do that now.

She drained the last of her coffee, peering over the rim of the mug to find Rick looking at her intently.

Her eyes met his, and her breath caught in her throat, making her nearly choke on the coffee.

Struggling to swallow it, she knew she wasn't imagining this. An image passed through her mind of kissing him, how his lips would feel against hers.

She fought off the image. Was she losing her mind? Was she so lonely she was focusing all these wild imaginings on Rick? It had to stop. Maybe if they did kiss, she'd see there was nothing between them but friendship.

The idea loomed temptingly.

But what was she going to do, ask him to kiss her?

And this was his fault. Why was he looking at her this way? He never had before. Had he?

She stood up. The morning air hung hot and heavy and was threatening to smother her. Nervously, she smoothed her skirt. "I guess we'd better get going. There's no sense in taking two cars. Do you want to come with me?"

He shook his head, dark hair splaying across his forehead. "I'll drive." He tossed his keys in the air.

His car, a black Bonneville, was parked around the side. Tracy was surprised to see he had a phone in it.

"So I can keep in touch with the construction crews," he explained, noticing her looking at it.

Her eyes narrowed as he cranked the ignition. The air conditioner spit out a blast of tepid air. "It'll cool off in a minute," he promised.

"What exactly do you do for this construction company?" she asked.

"A little of everything," he said, backing around the drive.

The interior of the car smelled of leather and him.

"What's the name of it?" she pressed.

He hesitated. "I'm sure you've never heard of it."

"What's the name?"

"Evans Construction," he muttered.

"It's your company," she proclaimed. "Why didn't you tell me?"

"It's no big deal. I've been lucky. I didn't see any sense in flaunting it."

She leaned back in the seat. "You have changed. There was a time when we were never anything but honest with each other."

"There was, wasn't there? I didn't lie."

"You didn't tell the whole truth, either. There's a difference between working for a construction company and owning one, Rick. Did you think I'd be anything but happy for you?"

Rick watched the road, aware of the light scent of oranges and jasmine at his side, the rustling of her clothes. He could deliver some honesty right now that would really rock her.

"So you think you know me well enough that you can always guess the truth?" he asked.

"Sometimes," she said.

He pulled up in front of the furniture store, angle parking at the curb.

"And other times you see only what you want to see. Shannon had you blinded."

Her mouth dropped open indignantly as the car stopped.

"What's that mean?" she asked.

He turned to her, his expression hard. "He charmed you out of seeing how badly he treated you. He'd stand you up for a date, then the next day there he was smiling and joking and you clung to his every word. There were a lot of times I wanted to punch it out with him. If—"

He broke off his words and swung open the car door. "None of it matters anymore, anyway," he said. His eyes riveted back to her. "Just don't go through life denying yourself happiness and always thinking he was the one. Remember how it really was. He was my friend, too. But you know yourself if things had been right between the two of you, you would have stayed here and married him."

"He didn't want to hold me back."

"Sweetheart, he couldn't make the commitment."

Tears threatened. Tracy knew there was a lot of truth in Rick's stabbing words. But it was hard to accept something she'd refused to acknowledge all these years.

Maybe some secret part of her had held out hope that Shannon would change, that someday they'd find each other again. It was startling to discover that had ended long before Shannon's death. She reached for the door handle.

"Do you have to be so brutal?" she accused. "Why? Why not just let it go?"

"Because it's something I should have said a long time ago instead of watching you suffer. There's more—"

"No. We'd better go inside."

After a stormy start, the morning dragged along. Rick disappeared upstairs into the loft, and Tracy was glad for the lull.

Why did he keep attacking her, battering her with truths and expectations? He hadn't been like this before, she reflected. He'd been quiet and accepting. More accepting of her, anyway. Now he was acting almost as though he wanted to hurt her, sever their friendship.

She sighed, glancing around the spacious showroom. She certainly couldn't figure it out.

She wondered what she was supposed to do. Deciding to familiarize herself with the merchandise, she spent the good part of half an hour browsing through rows of intriguing unique pieces of furniture—a child-size wicker rocker, a rolltop desk Hank would have killed for.

Realizing she knew little about furniture in general, she decided to scan the files for descriptions of the pieces. Maybe if she was lucky, no customers would come in until after Shannon's cousin Sam arrived and took over.

She chided herself for being a coward. She could handle this. Hadn't she had the guts to walk into the biggest station in Dallas and ask for a job? And gotten it! She could sell furniture if she had to. And contrary to what Rick believed, she wasn't a quitter.

She glanced up at the loft, unable to see him, and wondered what he was doing up there. Probably napping on one of the bunk beds, she told herself, still irritated with him.

They'd never used to argue. Had they both changed so much they couldn't stand each other anymore? Why hadn't he told her he owned a company? Had he thought she would be anything but happy for him?

She sighed. Spotting a coffeemaker, she decided to put on a pot before she tackled the files. Just as she got it going, the front door opened, and a hefty young man in cutoffs and a faded T-shirt entered.

Tracy paled. A customer.

She forced a smile. "Hi! Can I help you?"

He approached her timidly, looking her up and down. "I'm George."

She paused, waiting for more. Forcing her smile to stay in place, she said finally, "Nice to meet you, George. Can I help you?"

He pursed his lips. "I work here. I do still work here, don't I?" he asked.

Tracy gasped with sudden understanding. Cilla

hadn't mentioned employees, but of course there had to be some.

"What do you do?" she asked.

"Whatever Mr.—I did whatever Mr. Roberts told me to."

Tracy blinked.

Remembering her manners, she smiled and extended her hand. "I'm Tracy Madison. I was a friend of Mr. Roberts, and I'll be in charge until his cousin arrives at the end of the week."

He shook her proffered hand lightly. "Yes, ma'am. I know who you are. I saw you at the funeral. Everybody in Cherry Cove knows who you are."

Tracy felt herself blushing.

"Would you like a cup of coffee?"

"No, thank you. I don't drink coffee. I'd rather just go to work."

Tracy wondered why Cilla hadn't told her and Rick that Shannon had a strapping young man working for him who looked as if he could lift a chest of drawers one-handed. She wondered if any other employees were going to show up.

She drummed her nails against the desk top. "Go up in the loft," she instructed. "There's a man up there named Rick. He'll tell you what to do."

George nodded. "He's probably making room for the furniture shipment that's due in this afternoon."

Her eyebrows shot up.

"How much furniture?" she asked, her throat tight.

George shrugged. "Mr. Roberts always bought a lot at once."

"Do me a favor and tell Rick that," she asked.

George nodded before heading upstairs.

Tracy eyed the desk chair and resisted the urge to collapse in it. This wasn't going to be as easy as she thought.

Don't panic, she told herself.

She filled a Styrofoam cup with coffee, then turned calmly to the desk. Shannon's desk.

There was no time now for sentiment or sadness, she reminded herself. She had business to tend to.

Hoping to find a clue to what she was doing, she flipped through the files in the drawer. Giving up shortly, she reached for the phone and dialed Cilla's number.

"Cilla," she said, thankful the old woman was at home. "I hate to bother you, but I'm at the store, and I'm having trouble sorting things out."

"I never had much to do with the store's daily operation, but I'll help you all I can."

"George is here. Are there any other employees? Do they know the store is open?"

She turned at the sound of rustling behind her and saw Rick at the coffeemaker filling a cup.

She shot him a panic-stricken glance.

With a shrug, he raised the white cup in a mock toast and headed back up to the loft.

Cilla's answer came slowly over the phone line. "There is a salesclerk."

Tracy clutched her chest in relief. "What time does she come in?"

"I think she only came in when Shannon called and asked her to. She's a retired teacher—Pearl Harding."

"Mrs. Harding is selling furniture?" Tracy stifled a giggle. Mrs. Harding had been her math teacher in seventh grade. The woman must be ninety by now, she calculated.

"Shannon said she was very good at it."

"Anyone else?"

"No. Shannon did most of it himself."

"Do you know anything about a furniture shipment coming in this afternoon?"

"Mercy, no. Is one coming?"

Tracy raked a hand through her curls in frustration. "He never said anything about how much he bought?"

During a poignant silence, Tracy dared to hope Cilla would remember something.

"He always bought a lot at one time," she said.

Tracy's hope evaporated. "Okay. Thanks, anyway. Are you okay, Cilla?"

"I'll be all right," she said, her voice sounding

faraway. "Hold on and I'll give you Mrs. Harding's number. I'm sure she'll be glad to help out."

No sooner had Tracy finished scribbling the number on a notepad than a clanging over the front door announced the arrival of a thirtyish couple in canvas slacks and knit shirts boasting designer logos.

She braced herself. These were real customers. It was going to be a long day, and it had only just begun.

The clock on the wall showed one giant minute until five.

"Thank you so much for coming in, Mrs. Harding," Tracy told the small, prim woman, who had turned out to be younger than ninety, after all. "I can't tell you how much I appreciate everything you've done today. You will be back tomorrow, won't you?"

"Stop worrying, Tracy. I'll come in as long as you need me. Gives me a chance to get out of the house. I get tired of sitting around staring at the cat."

"I don't know how I would have managed without you." She meant it.

The couple who came in before the former teacher had arrived were passing through on their way from Fort Worth, and they had recognized Tracy immediately from her show. Selling them furniture had been almost too easy, but Tracy found herself lost when it came to writing up the receipt and figuring sales tax.

While she'd stood there fumbling through the receipt book, Rick had materialized at her side like magic, handling the business end of it as though he did this every day.

After he and George loaded the couple's new desk in the back of their van, Rick had showed her how to decipher the microscopic print on the sales-tax tables, patiently explaining what she needed to include on the receipt.

His arm had brushed hers, and she found herself marveling at the warm, clean smell of him instead of concentrating. The experience left her drained and unnerved. Why was Rick, of all people, having this effect on her?

Now, she said good night to Mrs. Harding, who reminded her for the tenth time she'd always predicted Tracy would go far one day. Tracy didn't share that particular memory. The class was math—her worst, and as she remembered it, the prediction was she'd never be able to balance her own checkbook, which wasn't far from the truth. Still, she smiled and nodded, not contradicting the woman. Mrs. Harding must have her mixed up with one of her other former students.

Happily, she turned the Closed sign to face the sidewalk, stifling the impulse to jump for joy.

She wondered where Rick had disappeared to.

Since they'd come together, she couldn't leave without him unless she wanted to walk home. She didn't.

She ventured out on the dock, where she found George and Rick, stripped of his shirt, sliding the last of the sofas inside the warehouse.

"We can worry about where to display it tomorrow," Rick told George.

Tracy was unable to avoid inspecting his muscles. His skin was beaded with sweat, and she realized guiltily he'd been doing hard manual labor all afternoon.

"See you tomorrow, Rick," George said, jumping off the side of the dock and heading across the alley.

"Good night, George," Tracy called.

Rick turned and found his shirt on one of the sofas.

"Nice kid," Rick said. "He plays quarterback on the high school team." He pulled the shirt on.

Tracy sank down on the nearest sofa. "This has been one wild day. I'm going to ask Cilla for Sam's phone number and personally call and beg him to get here early."

She threw her hands in the air. "I thought this would be easy."

Rick laughed softly, appraising her. The crisp white blouse hung limply over her, clinging and wrinkled. She'd ditched the blazer to her suit hours ago. He sat down beside her, gazing out into the alley. "I guess I'd better close this back door. I take it you're ready to leave."

"I was ready about six hours ago. I think I'll soak in the tub for about three hours. Then I'll be fine." Her eyes met his, and she grew aware of their sides touching.

Why and how did he have her feeling like a schoolgirl? This was not only puzzling—it was ridiculous, she affirmed.

"I guess you had the roughest day," she volunteered. "You're the one who needs to go home and relax."

"Not tonight. I've got to go to Houston and get some clothes and things to last the rest of the week."

"Tonight?" she asked, biting back a request to join him. Escaping from Cherry Cove and all the memories here loomed as a welcome respite.

Last night she'd had to ask to go walking with him. She refused to invite herself into his territory again.

He got up and swung the huge metal door shut with a clang, blocking out the sunlight and leaving them in semidarkness. He turned slowly back to her, projecting a powerful silhouette. "I'd appreciate some company if you can give up that long soak. I thought we could split a pizza."

A slow smile covered Tracy's lips. He knew her weakness for pepperoni pizza. He also knew it wasn't available in Cherry Cove.

"Is that a bribe?" she asked.

"It's a lonesome drive," he said.

"You really do want me to go, don't you?"

"You sound so surprised."

"After what you said earlier . . ."

"Forget what I said earlier. I was always a little jealous of Shannon."

Tracy nodded. Looking back, she couldn't blame him. Shannon got all the attention, all the opportunities.

"Can I stop by the house and change?"

"Of course. I fully intend to take a shower. But we do have to hurry. It's a two-hour drive, and we don't want to get back too late."

"So let's go," she agreed.

Falling into his good graces again washed away the lingering effects of a hard and terrible day.

Chapter Three

Rick sat on the front steps of the old Victorian bed-and-breakfast, refreshed from his shower and watching the evening sunlight streak across the landscape as he waited for Tracy.

He still wasn't sure what had possessed him to invite her to come with him. Maybe it was watching her struggle with the store today. Not many people would have done that to help an old lady.

At the sound of the screen door opening, he turned and saw Tracy emerge, grinning, through the front door. She was wearing light-blue jeans that hugged her figure, a western-cut shirt embroidered with cacti and beige-colored boots.

"Ready," she announced.

"Cute," he said, inspecting her and contrasting

her image with the career-girl look of this morning. "Are you always in costume?"

"I try to dress for the occasion," she said, discomforted by his scrutiny. "Let's go. I'm anxious for that pizza."

She led the way to his car parked over at the side of the house.

Rick drove silently until they were outside the city limits. Tracy sank back against the plush upholstered seat and sighed deeply.

"What was that for?" he asked.

"I'm glad you asked me to come with you. I was beginning to worry that maybe we weren't still friends. I want us to stay friends, Rick."

Rick felt his muscles tighten. Under the circumstances, they couldn't, really. Not the way she wanted. His feelings about her were too strong. Over the past day, he'd come to the conclusion he was going to have to lay his cards on the table or just make a break of it and walk away.

Years ago he'd been able to sit back silently and wait for whatever came. But he wasn't like that now. You didn't build a company by sitting around and waiting for things to happen. The things that happened on their own were usually bad, anyway. After his father had lost his job and been forced to uproot their family, he'd vowed he'd never be victimized that way.

"Surely you have friends in Dallas," he suggested.

"Not the same kind of friends. You're my connection to who I really am."

He rubbed his chin absently. "Then you should listen to me about not giving up your career. It's what you've always been about."

She gazed out the window at the passing landscape. "Someone from Western Broadcasting was at the station a few weeks ago. He watched me taping, then asked me a lot of questions later. He asked if I'd be opposed to moving to New York. Nothing will probably come of it."

"Doesn't sound like nothing to me. It's what you've always wanted."

"I guess in a way you're right—I am scared."

"You shouldn't be. You'll knock their socks off."

She toyed with the chain on her purse. "Not scared so much of failing, or even moving to a city full of strangers. I'm afraid of losing myself to it. Does that make any sense?"

Rick nodded. For the past several years he'd intentionally buried himself in his work. To him, it was an escape, and not one without rewards. Coming back to Cherry Cove, it was all catching up to him, all the things he'd shut out of his life because wanting something and not having it was too painful to dwell on.

"Success doesn't come cheap," he said.

She nodded. "I guess not. How about you? You must have given up a lot to build your company."

"Not really. The hardest part now is backing off and realizing I don't have to get out there and pick up a hammer and saw anymore. Leaves you feeling kind of restless, like a child that stops needing you."

"No regrets?"

"Not about my work." Sadness tinged his voice, and Tracy wondered what loss he had suffered over the years that he was thinking about now.

Silence iced the distance between them until Rick snapped out of his reflections.

He smiled. "How about Mrs. Harding?" he asked. "She certainly has mellowed. Used to run her class like a drill sergeant."

Tracy's ensuing laugh was light and clear. Within minutes, they were talking about their adventures in school, and a quiet contentment settled over her as some of the old easiness between her and Rick returned.

The time passed quickly, and soon after darkness fell, she saw on the horizon the towering, brightly lit oasis that was downtown Houston.

"Hold on, darlin'," Rick warned as he moved into the quickly moving traffic.

Tracy studied the passing cars, the urban landscape, as Rick maneuvered the car through the cutthroat highway traffic.

"Where do you live?" she asked.

"It's not far," he promised.

Soon he wound off the freeway into a neighborhood of older but well-tended brick homes with small, square lawns. He pulled up in the driveway of one.

"Home sweet home," he announced, killing the ignition.

"I love it," Tracy declared. "You have a whole house all to yourself."

"Well, almost," he said, leading her to the side door. "I have a roommate named Cecil."

"Cecil?" she asked.

As Rick shuffled through his keys, she heard a dog barking inside.

"You left your poor dog shut up all this time?" she asked incredulously.

"Of course not. The neighbor's been letting him out and feeding him."

He opened the door, and a dog that looked like a mop come to life bounded out, sniffing at Tracy's heels, then at Rick's.

Rick reached down and patted the animal's head. "Okay, behave yourself. We have company," he said.

The dog happily followed them inside the house. "He's just a mutt, but he's well-behaved. He loves to ride in the car and help me check out construction sites."

"Where did you get him?"

"Some upstanding citizen dumped off a box of puppies at an apartment complex we were working on. By the time I found them, the others were all dead."

He flicked on the lights.

Tracy surveyed her surroundings approvingly. They were in the kitchen. Everything was simple, functional, and incredibly neat and clean. She'd never thought much before about what a well-organized person Rick was.

"Do you want something to drink?" he asked.

"A soft drink would be nice," she said.

He opened the refrigerator, pulling out two canned sodas and handing her one.

"Thanks," she said.

Here in his environment, his presence loomed powerfully, filling her senses. She didn't think she'd ever been so aware of him before, and it was an odd, almost annoying feeling that made her uncharacteristically shy.

"Make yourself comfortable," he offered, gesturing toward the living room. "It will only take a few minutes for me to throw what I need in a suitcase."

Soft drink in hand, Tracy wandered into the living room. Cecil followed close at her heels. He looked down the hall in the direction Rick had disappeared, apparently debating who he should follow. Finally, he curled up on the floor beside the sofa, apparently deciding to keep an eye on her.

Tracy took a swig of the canned cola, savoring its coldness. After the long ride, she didn't feel like sitting down. She paced the room, looking over photographs of Rick's family, amazed at how everyone had changed, how grown up Billy looked in his graduation picture.

She studied a watercolor hanging on the wall, surprised to see it was an original. She hadn't known Rick collected art. But then, she was quickly learning there were many things she didn't know about Rick.

She looked at the curlicue signature in the bottom corner. M. Henson. No one she knew.

Restlessly, she called to Rick, "Can I take the dog out?"

"Straight down the hall to the back door," he called back. "He'll go out in the yard."

"Come on, Cecil," she urged, starting down the hall, surprised the dog actually followed her.

The dog ambled out into the yard, and Tracy followed, walking the length of the small fenced enclosure with him.

About five minutes later she went back inside, surprised to hear voices in the kitchen.

Curiously, she stepped into the room and found Rick standing beside the table, talking to a woman dressed in sandals, cutoffs, and a sleeveless cotton shirt. A mane of long brown hair tumbled down her back.

"Hi!" the smiling woman greeted her. "I'm Miriam Henson, Rick's dog sitter. I live next door."

Dumbfounded, Tracy stared at the friendly young woman, suddenly feeling very possessive of Rick. Stark, green jealousy was what she felt, she realized. And she had no right, no reason to. What was wrong with her?

She returned Miriam's smile. "I'm Tracy Madison," she said, extending her hand.

Miriam shook it. "I thought Rick was making it up when he said he knew you. We get your show on cable."

"Miriam's an artist," Rick said.

Miriam shrugged modestly. "Actually, I'm an unemployed college graduate. I'm staying next door with my parents until I find something."

"You did the watercolor in the living room," Tracy said, making the connection.

And she also made the connection of the close relationship between Miriam and Rick. Miriam had given him a painting, kept a key to his house, and took care of his dog.

Tracy felt like an intruder. She wondered, for the first time, if Rick had felt this way when she and Shannon had been dating.

She knew she was being unreasonable. She had

no claim on Rick. Of course, he had his own life. The richer it was, the happier she should be.

"The bad news is," Rick was saying to Miriam now, "I'm going to be staying in Cherry Cove for the rest of the week."

Miriam's eyes darted to Tracy, then quickly back to Rick. Despite her unfaltering smile, Tracy knew in that instant that whatever their relationship, Miriam harbored some strong feelings for Rick.

And why not? He was good-looking, successful, gentle, and strong. A person would have to be a fool to overlook that.

And yet she always had.

Conflicting emotions whirled through her. She knew she was drawn to Rick. She'd thought it was because they were old friends, but now she suspected something else was at work here.

Miriam smiled up at Rick. "I'll just take Cecil home with me then. He's not any trouble. My parents even like him."

She called the dog.

"Thanks," Rick said. "I'll call you when I get back."

"Nice to meet you," Tracy said, watching her go.

"Likewise," Miriam replied.

The side door closed.

"I'll get my suitcase," Rick said. "I'll just be a minute."

* * *

Country music blared from a jukebox as Tracy and Rick wove their way through the crowded pizza parlor, trying to keep up with the hostess who was leading them to a table. Rick's hand rested lightly against Tracy's waist.

Heat rose to her face as she remained aware of the slight pressure. She was still trying to unravel the mystery of her strong and slightly out-of-kilter reactions to Rick's every move. The answer was obvious, she'd resolved. Somehow she'd mixed up the memories of Shannon and Rick's presence in her mind.

After all, a first love was something you never completely got over. And Shannon's death had evoked a torrent of memories.

The thought left her empty. She was tired. And very hungry.

The hostess stopped and gestured toward a booth so recently vacated, the tabletop was still damp. Tracy slid into the seat gratefully.

A waitress appeared as quickly as the hostess left, set two menus down, and smiled broadly at Rick.

She's flirting with him, Tracy realized. She took a second look at Rick herself. Although he had never displayed any of Shannon's easy, outgoing spirit, he presented a handsome, powerful figure. Naturally, women would flirt with him.

The realization made her uneasy. Was she so jealous of a friend, she hated the thought of women throwing themselves at him? She knew she was being unreasonable, and the worst part was, she couldn't help it.

"What's wrong?" Rick asked from the opposite side of the table, catching her perplexed expression.

"Nothing," she replied quickly, reaching for the menu. "Do you come here often?"

"Once in a while."

She narrowed her eyes. "If I remember correctly, you never shared my passion for good pizza." Her expression softened. "I'd forgotten. We could have gone somewhere else, Rick."

"I promised you pizza," he insisted. "You'll have pizza."

She was too tired to argue with him. But she felt she didn't deserve his being so nice to her.

"Is it always this crowded?" she asked. She wondered who he came here with. Miriam? Or were there others?

The waitress approached the table again, her order pad poised. She stared openly at Tracy.

"Aren't you on the Dallas cable show?" she asked finally.

"Yes," Tracy admitted.

The girl's eyes widened. "Wait until I tell my mom you really do wear glasses. She says they're stage props, without lenses in them." She turned to

Rick, gazing at him curiously. Tracy realized she was only about sixteen.

"And who are you?" she finally blurted, and at Rick's stunned expression, it was all Tracy could do to keep from laughing.

"My name is Rick Evans, and I'm not on television," he finally said.

The girl's expression fell. "Oh. Can I take your order?"

He ordered pizza with double pepperoni, antipasto and iced tea.

After she was gone, he looked at Tracy. "Does this happen to you everywhere you go?" he asked.

She shook her head. "Only once in a while at home. I didn't expect it here."

"It will be hard to have a normal life once you're on the networks."

Tracy rearranged her silverware. "I used to think a so-called normal life was the last thing I wanted. Now it's starting to sound pretty good."

He shook his head. "You'd be bored silly with anything less than what you've been working for. Some people were just meant for special things."

"Do you really believe that, that some things are meant to be a certain way?"

He looked thoughtful. "Yes, but that doesn't mean they'll just happen on their own. I wouldn't have my own company if I hadn't planned it every step of the way."

"Maybe not everyone is as strong as you are."

"You're strong, Tracy. You always have been."

"Because I always had you there to keep me from falling apart."

"I wasn't around when you managed to walk away from Cherry Cove or land your own television show. I'd say you manage pretty well on your own."

"You know, it always seemed like the three of us needed each other so much. And yet it turned out we didn't."

His expression changed, and she couldn't read it.

"I would have been lost in Shannon's shadow if I'd stayed in Cherry Cove. You would have, too."

"That's not fair."

"Isn't it? It doesn't mean Shannon wasn't a great guy. But I didn't want to go through life on his coattails. He was the football star, the captain of the debating team. He'd smile at a teacher and get an automatic A. I'd get a C because I'd walked in the door behind him."

"Why didn't you ever say anything, do anything?"

"He and I were always competing, Tracy. You just never saw it. You were too wrapped up in him."

"It's funny," she observed. "He was always jealous of you."

His eyebrows jetted upward. "How?"

"You had a family. All he had was his grandmother. He said you were smarter than he was and patient while he was impulsive."

Rick remained unconvinced. "Why didn't he ever mention those things?"

Tracy shrugged. "You said the two of you were always competing. No one likes to reveal his weaknesses to a rival."

Relief washed through her as the waitress appeared with their drinks and food. She'd always liked to believe high school had been such an uncomplicated time in her life. Now Rick was forcing her to see it hadn't been.

Rick, too, was ready to change the subject. "What did you think of my painting?" he asked as he dished up pizza.

"Miriam's watercolor?" she asked.

"Uh-huh." He tried to break a long, stubborn string of mozzarella.

"She's very talented. It was generous of her to give it to you."

"Actually, I bought it from her." He slid a piece of steaming pizza in front of her. "She's getting anxious about not being able to find a job right off, and she helps me with Cecil and picking up the mail."

"Generous of you then," she said, alarmed at the comfort she felt at the knowledge he wasn't accepting gifts from his attractive young neighbor and admirer.

She looked across the table and saw Rick, absorbed in his food. Suddenly she grew fascinated with the lines of his face, familiar yet new and intriguing. Who was this man she'd thought she knew so well?

Rick's head lifted, and his eyes lit unexpectedly on her. She felt a guilty constriction in her throat. But something prevented her from tearing her eyes away immediately. A deep-seated thrill coursed through her as she continued to meet his gaze.

Rick smiled, one of his trademark long, slow grins. And all at once her heart was spinning. He winked at her.

What did he have to do that for? she wondered as her pulse got threadier. Coming here was a mistake. Everything was so mixed up in her mind, she feared if she didn't get a grip on her reactions soon, something foolish would happen and she'd lose one of the best friends she'd ever had.

"Aren't you hungry?" Rick asked, gesturing at the untouched food before her.

Obligingly, she reached for her fork, although her appetite had diminished. Yes, she reflected silently. She was hungry, but for something that had been missing from her life for a very long time.

Rick steered the car down the darkened highway, listening to the soft drone of the car stereo on low volume. Every star in the sky was visible tonight.

Alone with his thoughts, he inhaled the subtle, citrusy scent that haunted him.

But right now the fragrance was quite real. He chanced a sidewise glance at the figure dozing in the passenger seat beside him. Her face was relaxed, angelic. A pulse throbbed in her neck, and her chest moved evenly as she breathed.

She was more beautiful now than he remembered, even with the silly nail polish. Secretly, he'd hoped she'd fall short of his expectations.

Hadn't he known, he admonished himself, that she'd run to the creek after the funeral? He could have predicted it with the same precision he could cut boards and turn a blueprint into reality. And hadn't he been hoping to see her, be there to comfort her?

It had always been that way. He'd been around when he knew she'd need him, hoping one day she'd look up and discover she loved him, not Shannon. But it hadn't ever happened.

He loathed the deception. Long ago, he'd been afraid, afraid Shannon would beat him out of the running. Now he was afraid because . . .

Because she was too upset about Shannon?

Because she was headed for a career that didn't leave room in her life for anything else?

Because if her feelings for him went beyond friendship, she would have told him on her own.

He glanced at the sleeping form again. He'd met

other women who were beautiful, intelligent, sensitive. But none had her drive, her spunk, her aura. She was the woman he wanted to spend the rest of his life with. No other. And if his life meant anything at all, he would tell her before this week was out.

But he wouldn't rush it. All in good time.

Suddenly his smooth-riding car was wobbly and thumping. He wrestled it to the shoulder, killing the engine with a curse.

Carefully, he got out and inspected the back tire. As he suspected, it was flat.

The stop awoke Tracy. She opened her eyes to find the driver's seat empty, the door open, and the car surrounded by darkness.

Groggily, she pushed herself up in the seat.

Rick stuck his head inside the door frame, retrieving his keys from the ignition.

She looked at him inquiringly.

"Flat tire," he informed her. "Go back to sleep. I'll have it fixed in a minute."

"I can help," she volunteered, grabbing the door handle and opening the door. She got out and met him around the back of the car as he was opening the trunk.

"It's under control," he said. She was standing so close to him, and he hadn't been able to think about much else except her being in the car for the past hour and a half.

"I can't just stand here," she insisted, throwing

her hands up in the air. "I do know how to change a tire."

He looked her up and down evenly. "You don't have to prove anything here," he said. "Just let me fix it." He plunked a lantern into her hands. "You can set this out back there so I won't get hit by any oncoming cars."

Miffed, she took the lantern, turned on the flasher, and set it several feet behind the car. She wasn't trying to prove anything. She just wanted to be useful.

She paced the edge of the woods, listening to sounds of Rick jacking up the car, twisting off the lugnuts.

Rick struggled with the tire. The last thing he needed was to get stranded with Tracy in some unpopulated area. Being with her and not being able to touch her the way he wanted, tell her how he felt was driving him wild.

Just as he was nearly finished putting on the temporary tire, he felt her presence behind him. *What now?* he thought with a rush of impatience.

Ignoring her, he lowered the car.

The voice attacked him like a cold wind. "You don't have to prove anything here. Just let me fix it," she mocked him.

He looked up and saw her standing over him with her hands on her hips, her chin jutting out at him, daring him.

Coolly, he appraised her, a light coming to his eyes.

"What is this? A rebellion?"

Tracy nodded.

Rick stood.

She laughed. "I've never seen you get so huffy before. What's the matter with you?"

He laughed, taking a step closer. "Just tired, I guess. Angry about the tire. I didn't mean to take it out on you."

She nodded. "Will we make it home?"

"Slowly. It would be best if we found a station open where we could get a real tire, but I'm not counting on it. Not out here at this time of night."

He knew he needed to put the tools back in the trunk, but he couldn't take his eyes off her. The moonlight highlighted her small, smooth features, giving her face an ethereal quality.

"Tracy . . ." he began.

She looked so trusting. She had no idea, he reminded himself.

He took another step closer.

Tracy continued to meet his gaze.

At his growing closeness, her heart throbbed, beating so hard it almost hurt. Everything out here was so unreal. There was no past, no outside world. Like a cat paralyzed in oncoming headlights, she couldn't move away.

One more step, and his chest was nearly against hers.

She looked up into his face, her lips parting slightly.

If she didn't know better . . .

His hand grazed her neck, such tenderness in his fingertips, she trembled beneath his touch, closing her eyes.

Her mind raced dizzily. She knew she should be surprised by this, yet somehow she wasn't. She knew she shouldn't want this, but she did. More than she had any right to.

His hands covered her shoulders, and he moved over her, pulling her closer. She felt the full force of his quiet power, and, in contrast, she grew weak in the ankles, liquid and pliant.

Her heart threatened to burst as his lips closed in on hers, and his name slipped out quietly before her world spun into sweetness and syrup.

Her arms reached out to him, wrapped around his chest as she clung to him.

She couldn't think and didn't want to. Time, even the wind, had ceased.

He drew back, leaving her breathless.

All at once, the tenderness in his eyes disappeared, replaced by a look of shock.

"Trace, I'm sorry," he said, releasing her. So much for patience. This was exactly what he'd feared he would do.

His expression was so apologetic, as though he'd hurt her instead of kissing her as no one ever had before.

Still breathless, she stared at him in confusion. Why was he sorry? Should she be?

"No harm done," she said, struggling to regain her composure. He'd only swept her feet off the ground just to set them back hard. She moved back. Why was he tormenting her this way? "We'd better go," she said.

Unable to look at him any longer, she headed off to retrieve the lantern. A tear she couldn't explain stung her cheek, and she surreptitiously wiped it with her finger.

She tossed the lantern in the trunk, not looking at Rick who stood waiting to close the lid.

He spotted the wet stain on her face, and guilt purged him. Now he'd done it, he reasoned. He'd made her cry. It was a heck of a way to treat the woman he loved.

Chapter Four

"Where's Tracy?" Rick asked the next morning, his gaze sweeping through the deserted kitchen.

"Tore off outside with her coffee," Alice answered with a shrug, handing him a filled mug.

He accepted it and headed toward the back door. "Thanks," he said absently.

"You're welcome," Alice said to the now empty doorway. She shook her head and sighed deeply. Long ago she had noticed how Rick and Tracy seemed to always be together, how good they looked side-by-side, the easy way they talked and kidded around.

Even back then, she'd suspected they'd be together one day. But she'd made a policy of staying out of the situation, keeping her opinions to herself.

Her daughter seemed to idolize Shannon. He had been a nice boy, she thought sadly. But too self-absorbed for her liking. In her mind, Shannon had never been right for her only daughter. But in the murky aftermath of tragedy, Tracy seemed to have forgotten how much pain he'd caused her.

This morning Tracy's abrupt withdrawal and Rick's shadowed eyes told her something was going on between them. Maybe they didn't understand it, but she did. She just hoped Tracy was going to be strong enough to deal with it.

At first, Rick couldn't see her. His eyes swept over the long, vacant porch, then trailed to the woods. He spotted her there, propped against a tree, staring off toward the field beyond. Although she held her coffee cup suspended in front of her, he never saw her raise it to her lips.

Rick noticed she'd ditched her previous day's office attire for a white cotton shirt tucked into a pair of jeans, dark sunglasses masking her eyes.

What was she thinking about as she stared off across the Texas countryside? he wondered. Was she blaming him for their encounter last night? In retrospect, he tasted the soft moistness of her lips. And he felt anew the fervor with which she'd returned his kiss.

That was something he hadn't imagined, and it gave him hope.

He shouldn't have apologized. He wasn't sorry it had happened. That kiss was something he had wanted and waited for a long time.

But he decided to tread softly. He didn't want to push her into pushing him away. Something he seemed to be very good at.

The air, still slightly cool from the night, smelled fresh and wild from the foliage. Everything was still except for the chirping of birds and rustling of small animals.

He descended the porch steps and walked across the dew-dampened grass toward her.

"Tracy?" he said in a low voice, not wanting to alarm her.

"Good morning, Rick," she greeted him as she turned, as if she'd sensed all along he was there.

He felt her eyes upon him, even though he couldn't see them through the dark glasses, couldn't tell whether they were welcoming him or accusing him.

And even in the light of morning, he longed to reach out and trace her satiny lips with his fingertip. His glance lingered on the creamy smoothness of her throat, exposed in the V where her collar was unbuttoned.

He drew in a deep breath as her scent ignited the morning air.

"I thought you'd left without me," he said.

She shook her head. "There's no point in that,"

she admitted. "You know more about running a business than I do."

He took a hard look at her, wishing he could see what was behind those accursed glasses.

"I guess we'd better be getting along then," he ventured, turning back toward the porch.

She startled him by reaching out and catching hold of his arm.

He looked down at her questioningly, poignantly aware of her tentative grip on him, the warmth her small hand radiated. Even this slight contact set off sparks between them. Couldn't she feel the pull? Or didn't she want to?

"We've got to talk about what happened last night," she said, her glance wavering. "We've always talked about everything."

His expression sharpened. His eyes narrowed. "And you've never hidden behind spy glasses before," he pointed out dryly.

Slowly, Tracy removed her hand from his arm and reached up to remove the glasses.

The sight of her eyes, red and puffy, made him feel like a scoundrel.

"You're making far too much of this," he said quickly.

The only thing he'd done wrong was to care for her. And he didn't believe that was wrong. Still, if the prospect was so distressing to her she was mentally torturing herself, he wasn't going to press it.

Pouring out his feelings was useless if his confession would hurt her in some way.

Tracy held her gaze on him, trying not to falter as he minimized what had happened as quickly as a doctor would dismiss a hangnail.

If he had admitted he cared about her in a way she was starting to suspect she cared about him, she could deal with it from there. But to attribute a kiss that had touched a tender, secret place in her heart to nothing more than a dark night and country road made no sense at all.

She raised her chin. Looking at him now, harsh and handsome in the sunlight, she remembered her unexpected reaction to his closeness last night, like stepping inside a house she'd been looking at from only the outside all her life. And then the sweet, raging surprise that struck her like heat lightning, leaving her simultaneously giddy and frightened.

In a way, she yearned for their innocent friendship. But after last night, she knew that could never be recaptured. Everything had changed, and a wall had gone up between them and their past.

Had she been foolish enough to halfway hope he'd say he had kissed her because he was feeling these new things, too? Well, she certainly wasn't going to ruin what was left of their friendship by disclosing her own disturbing feelings.

"I think I'm allergic to all this overgrowth," she replied, quickly replacing the glasses.

Rick nodded, but he knew she'd never been allergic to anything in her life.

"Good," he said. "Not good that you have allergies. Good that you're not upset about last night."

She slipped her hands behind her back. "I was caught by surprise. I think we both were."

"Yes," he agreed.

She shrugged stiffly. "I suppose that was bound to happen sooner or later," she speculated. "I guess it was something we just had to do. Really, it's amazing that never happened years ago."

Had it not been for Shannon, it would have, Rick reflected. And she was describing their encounter as though it had been a science experiment. He chided himself for being such a coward and not revealing the truth as he planned. But he wouldn't if it was only going to worry her.

Still, he began feeling angry with himself, with her.

"I wouldn't want it to change things between us," she said, knowing a part of her, that tiny spot in her heart that was suddenly alive and needful, wanted everything to change.

"Of course not," Rick bit back, pouring his untouched coffee onto the ground. "Don't give it another thought. I'll be by the car when you're ready."

He turned on the heel of his boot and walked off. Listening to the drumming of his footsteps as he marched across the porch planks, she shivered involuntarily.

What had she done? Everything had always been so easy between the two of them, and suddenly their relationship was strained and difficult.

She didn't understand, but she believed it was her fault. She was the one who was suddenly seeing him differently.

Certainly, she hadn't shied away from his kiss last night. Yet it was he who had initiated it. It was he who had held her as though she were made of spun gold.

Why? she wondered. Was he trying, through her, to resolve his past? Or was he just trying to drive her mad?

She copied his earlier motion, spilling the contents of her coffee cup over the puddle on the ground where he'd drained his.

Most mystifying to her was why this had never happened before. But the answer popped into her mind almost the instant the question did. Shannon. She'd been so infatuated with him.

Guiltily, she realized she hadn't thought about Shannon since yesterday.

Rick spent the morning in the loft, moving furniture to make room for the new stock that came in. But he kept a quiet eye on Tracy, enjoying the way she moved as she found her bearings in the store.

She flashed customers a friendly smile, shook hands with them, and obligingly signed the occasional autograph that was requested. He watched George and somber Mrs. Harding buckle under to Tracy's charm as she lavished them with generous praise for even the simplest tasks and asked with genuine interest about their lives outside the store.

When a toddler cried in protest as her parents were about to leave the store, Tracy searched the aisles to locate the cloth doll the girl had dropped.

He wondered if she was aware of the power she had over people. Part of the danger was that she looked like an unassuming country girl, not a glamorous television star. And she cared about other people, maybe too much for her own good.

He remembered her grave concern when his sister, Gina, had undergone an emergency appendectomy. It was as though she'd suffered the pain herself.

Acknowledging this, he felt a little miffed that he alone was shut out from her circle of concern. She seemed tuned in to everyone's feelings except his.

As he shoved one end of a sofa into place, he wondered what he was going to do about her. The safest move would be to go back to Houston and try once again to forget.

But he thought of his empty house and his quiet life. Cecil made a good companion, but he needed much more than a dog in his life.

Yet if he stayed, what would happen? Sooner or

later he'd tell her the truth. Sooner or later he wouldn't be able to resist kissing her again. He couldn't keep on telling her it didn't mean anything. She wasn't stupid.

Suddenly she materialized on the top of the steps. His eyes widened appreciatively.

She held out a sandwich, a bag of chips, and a Styrofoam cup with a straw sticking out of it.

"It's hot up here," she noted. "Why don't you come downstairs and eat in Shannon's office with us? The air-conditioning works better in there."

He stepped forward and accepted the proffered food. "I can get back to work faster if I just stay up here," he told her, inspecting the sandwich through the clear wrapping. "Thanks for the food, though."

"You're welcome," she said, holding her hands behind her back. She decided he was avoiding her, and the discovery saddened her. All morning long she had this panicky feeling he was going to leave and once again she'd be left alone in the midst of a relationship that had never quite materialized.

Was that what she wanted? she wondered with a start. Did she want Rick to be her lover? The outlandish thought excited her more than she wanted to admit.

"Enjoy your lunch," she said quickly and took off down the stairs like a spooked horse.

Rick wondered what he'd done this time.

* * *

After lunch, finding no more work to do in the loft, Rick drifted down to Shannon's office to look through his friend's books. He wanted to find out just what kind of financial shape Shannon had left Cilla in.

Always good with figures, he'd taken some night classes in accounting after he'd started his own business, figuring the more he knew, the less he had to rely on what others told him about his own affairs.

Hours later when he looked up and closed the fat ledger, it was nearly five-thirty. The store was quiet.

Cramped from sitting for such a long period, he stretched and scanned the deserted showroom. There was no sign of anyone. He knew George and Mrs. Harding must have left, but where was Tracy? Had she walked home and left him behind?

He hated the way they were suddenly skirting each other. Wouldn't it be better to just put the facts on the table and face them, no matter how it turned out?

"Tracy!" he called, his deep voice echoing through the building.

No answer came.

Somehow he knew she was there. He felt her presence.

Had something happened? Had she tried to move a piece of furniture and had it topple over on her?

Panicking, he raced to the back of the showroom, continuing to call her name.

When he finally heard her answer, her voice sounded small and far away.

"I'm up here," she said.

He scaled the stairs to the loft two at a time.

She was curled up on one corner of the sofa he'd moved earlier, her face red and tear-streaked.

"Why didn't you answer?" he demanded. His heart continued pounding even though he could see she was unharmed.

"I didn't want you to see me like this," she replied sullenly.

"I was afraid something had happened to you," he admonished her, stepping closer. He leaned over her, noticing the piece of paper she held between trembling fingers. "Why are you crying?"

She held out the paper, and he saw it was a yellowed photograph of the three of them together; she was standing in the middle between him and Shannon.

"I found this in the desk drawer. It just suddenly made all this seem so real and terrible—" Her voice broke.

He dropped onto the couch beside her, gathering her into his arms, cradling her head against his chest. Fresh tears dampened his shirt. He rocked her softly.

Tracy leaned against him. Suddenly it was the old Rick again, and she was the old Tracy. There was no one else in the world with whom she'd let her guard down.

Rick held her patiently. He understood she was crying over more than a picture.

Finally, she was calm and still against him. His chest constricted at the bittersweet irony of holding her yet knowing she was still far away from him.

"I was just wondering," she said. "Why do some people die young and others go on?"

"What happened to Shannon was an accident."

"He was driving too fast."

"Everyone drives too fast at one time or another. The traffic lights malfunctioned. It was a bizarre occurrence."

"I found that picture, and just thinking he'd kept it all this time, yet we all walked away from each other . . . Well, isn't it strange to you, Rick? That we cared so much about each other and still felt connected, yet we never visited each other."

"Maybe it was too painful, knowing we could never go back to those earlier days. Maybe each of us knew it would never be the same."

But he knew he'd never wanted to. The old days hadn't been the best time of his life.

He eased her off of his chest, propping her face in the palms of his hands. "Were you crying because you loved Shannon?" he asked. It was vital that he know.

A thrill twisted through her at the intensity of his

gaze, his closeness. She felt a tinge of betrayal. Her comfortable old friend had transformed suddenly into this new, unpredictable stranger who had her senses soaring. Her heart hammered, and she felt a quickening inside her as she looked into those deep, dark eyes that looked at her in a way she'd never known.

"I thought so," she said.

His eyes locked in on hers, softening at her answer.

"Maybe if I did, everything would have been different," she continued.

"I don't understand."

His face hovered close over hers, their noses nearly touching.

"Shannon did ask me to stay here. He wanted me to marry him."

Rick's eyebrows flared.

"And you didn't?"

"It was at the last minute. I was packed and ready to go off to school the next day. I knew if I stayed, I'd always wonder what I could have accomplished . . . I never told anyone he'd asked me."

"Whether you stayed or left wouldn't have made the difference in whether he had his accident. You don't believe he'd be alive now if you had stayed, do you?"

"No. I don't think Shannon and I would have stayed together long. But I should have been able to love him the way I wanted to. Maybe I don't know as much about myself as I've always thought I did."

"If you feel guilty about not staying here with him, punishing yourself by staying here now isn't going to change the past."

"I know that. Life has to go on."

"And it will," he promised. Moving slowly over her, he removed her glasses, placing a kiss on her eyelid, then on the other. A warmth settled over her, and she opened her eyes to look at him with a new wonder.

The corner of his lip raised up, and she felt an overwhelming intimacy pass between them. He was as familiar as the earth beneath her feet, yet held promise as intriguing as the heavens.

She moved forward, meeting his lips as they neared hers and welcoming the swirling sensation that surged through her. His hands on her back were hot and firm, pulling her closer against him.

She closed her mind to her fears and sought to tell him this way about her feelings for him. She clutched his shoulders as though she were afraid to let go.

The distant ringing of the telephone downstairs jolted her back to reality. She broke free.

"The phone," she said breathlessly.

"Leave it," he replied.

She got up, racing off down the stairs to answer it.

Stunned, Rick watched her hurry off.

After she disappeared, he pounded a fist into the sofa cushion.

Downstairs, Tracy lifted the telephone receiver. "Hello?"

"Goodness, you sound as though you'd just run a marathon." It was Cilla's thin voice.

"We were . . . I was up in the loft, straightening up." She hated lying, especially to Cilla.

"I was afraid you'd left for the day. Is Rick still there?"

Tracy's eyes strayed toward the loft. "Yes. He's still here. Would you like to speak to him?"

"Oh, no. That's not necessary. You two have been so kind, I just wanted to invite you over for dinner tonight. Sorry it's at the last minute."

Tracy wanted right now to escape Rick's conquering presence and get off by herself to sort things out. But she couldn't see a way of declining Cilla's invitation without hurting the older woman's feelings. Besides, Shannon's grandmother needed more right now than just someone to tend her business.

"I'll be there. I don't know about Rick. I'll have to ask him."

"Well, tell him we're counting on both of you," Cilla said. "Is seven too early?"

"Seven will be fine."

"Good. I'll look forward to seeing you then."

Tracy replaced the receiver. She looked up at the loft and saw Rick staring down at her over the railing. He looked hurt, bewildered.

Well, he should, she thought. She sure as heck was.

He came down the stairs, holding out something in his hand. Her glasses, she realized. She'd left them upstairs.

"Cilla wants us to come for dinner," she announced, avoiding his eyes.

"We need to talk, Trace."

Her fingers brushed his as she reached for her glasses.

"I know that." She wiped her palms on her jeans. "But not now. I can't. Dinner's at seven."

She walked to the front door and shot out, not stopping beside his car parked out front.

Rick muttered a curse. Wasn't it just his luck to fall forever and irrevocably in love with a woman who had no idea what she wanted?

He turned off the lights and locked the door as he left.

He caught up with Tracy a few blocks away, walking as furiously as though demons from hell were after her.

He slowed the car at the roadside.

"You're acting foolish, Hotshot," he called out.

She turned, scowled. Then, seeming to realize he

was right, she silently approached the car and got into the passenger side.

"The last thing I'd ever want to do is hurt you," he said as he drove.

This was something she'd always known.

She looked at him sidewise. "Ditto," she said, crossing her arms.

A heavy silence followed as he suddenly realized maybe they were each far too afraid of hurting the other. How far would they go to avoid it?

Chapter Five

What is wrong with me? Tracy asked herself as she stood under the hot, steamy shower. A week ago she would have said she had her life under control. Now she was questioning every aspect of her emotions herself. And, especially, her relationship with Rick.

She kept ending up in his arms and found that far from unpleasant. Even now she tingled at the memory of his kiss. And she was beginning to realize what she was feeling was something unrelated to her grief over Shannon. Shannon was a distant memory. Rick figured strongly into the present.

Maybe she should stop fighting it and see what happened. Was she so afraid of that?

Shutting off the spray of water, she wrapped herself in a plush towel.

She smiled slightly to herself as she padded barefoot out of the bathroom and across the bedroom to the closet in search of something to wear tonight.

It wasn't that she'd never wanted to fall in love. Ever since she was about twelve years old, she'd expected the proverbial handsome prince to come along and sweep her off her feet. She'd always had a flair for the dramatic. Once, she'd thought Shannon met that image of a prince. Later she'd expected to encounter one in the broadcasting world. But she hadn't spent much time looking for him.

Most of the men she met were too shallow, too aware of their own good looks, or else they were absorbed in their careers, as she was. She'd written off her girlish fantasy as a silly dream. While she'd assumed other men paled beside her memories of Shannon, was it someone else she'd really been comparing them to all this time?

Could it be he'd been there all the time, and she'd just never paid attention?

She sighed deeply as she began to dress. In a few more days, Rick would be going back to Houston, and she would be on her way to Dallas. Was there any point to exploring their relationship, taking it beyond the point of friendship?

But it had already passed that point, and neither of them had been able to stop it any more than the

Midwesterners could have walled back the overflowing Mississippi River. If they had, Rick wouldn't have been kissing her when Cilla called this afternoon.

Suddenly she needed to know how Rick felt about this. Was he as bewildered as she was?

She put on a two-piece shorts set and a pair of sandals, brushing her hair dry and applying a slight bit of makeup. Finished, she inspected herself in the mirror. When you paraded your face across television screens every afternoon, your looks were fair game for public comment.

How many times had she been told or read in the newspaper that she looked like "the girl next door"? She'd been told that was part of her appeal.

Often, she longed for a more glamorous, mature look—high cheekbones and long, blond hair. After all, she was nearing thirty and didn't want to resemble everyone's teenage neighbor forever. But Hank had told her her brand of scrubbed good looks was more rare than a model's sleek poise.

She couldn't argue. As long as her appearance had helped her get where she wanted to be, she could live with it.

Now she leaned forward, surprised to see a glow in her face that hadn't been there before, despite her restless sleep last night and her earlier crying jag. Had anyone else noticed it? she wondered. Was it there because of Rick?

She knew it was. Just when everything had started to lose meaning for her, there he was. As always.

Giving her neck a final spritz of cologne, she hurried downstairs, wondering whether he'd gone on ahead or waited for her.

A calming warmth washed over her as she found him in the spacious living room, sitting on the sofa, twisting a small bouquet of carnations in his big hands as he talked rodeo with one of the bed-and-breakfast guests.

He was wearing a geometric print western-cut shirt, jeans, boots, and a Stetson, and Tracy was sure the man who was listening intently would go home and tell his friends about having met a real cowboy. No harm in that. It was good for her parents' business.

Rick raised his eyes and cast her a long, slow smile. She grinned at him.

She'd been foolish, she thought, to believe she could avoid him or her own feelings. They had a few short days left together, so she might as well enjoy them. She pushed away the thought of how much she would miss that smile of his.

Not wanting to interrupt the conversation, she went out on the front porch and sat in one of the rocking chairs, enjoying the soft breeze that had sprung up. She closed her eyes, basking in the touch of the wind against her skin.

She opened them quickly as she felt the heat of a human hand against her bare arm.

Rick was standing over her.

"You looked like you were about to go to sleep," he said. His hand circled her slender arm. Reluctantly he withdrew it.

"No. I was just relaxing. The air feels a little cooler."

He laughed lightly. "Only if you stand still."

She stared up at him. "You're the one who did all the hard work today. Are you sure you want to go?"

He nodded. "I want to see how Cilla's doing." He held up the bouquet in his hand. "I got her these."

While Tracy was touched by his thoughtful gesture, she felt a vague disappointment the flowers weren't for her. Not that she deserved them after the way she'd stormed off this afternoon.

"She'll love them," Tracy predicted.

"Why don't you hold them?" he suggested, shifting the bundle from one hand to another. "I feel sort of silly."

Tracy laughed and took charge of the flowers. "Wouldn't want to ruin your macho image," she assured him. "But only until we get there. You should give them to her."

"I guess we'd better go," he said, extending a hand to help her up.

Tracy looked up at him, feeling a fluttering inside when her eyes locked on his dark, intent ones. Although she was perfectly capable of rising on her own, she placed her hand in his and yielded to his strength as he pulled her upward.

His grip on her hand lingered as she stood just a few inches in front of him. His soapy masculine scent made her a little dizzy.

He clasped his free hand over hers. "I was afraid I'd upset you this afternoon."

Dark lashes fluttered over her wide eyes, and she met his gaze directly. "I'm not upset now," she said.

He favored her with a smile. "It was never my intention to make you angry."

And exactly what was your intention? she thought, her heart hammering wildly.

"I owe you an apology. I seem to save my stupid tears for you."

He shook his head. "They're not stupid. It's perfectly natural to cry. You and Shannon were close once. You've always been the kind of person who absorbs everyone else's pain. I don't know why you never admit to your own."

"With you I always have. I guess you're the only person I've ever felt safe with."

"I guess we've always pretty much understood each other."

"Until now," she said.

A long silence froze the air between them as they met each other's gaze.

"Ten years have gone by. That's a long time."

"I guess I expected everything to be the same when I saw you again. And it's not."

"That's not necessarily bad," he advised.

"No, it's wonderful I think. Maybe it's not so strange that we would feel differently about each other. I mean, we've both grown up. I'm beginning to understand I was more dazzled by Shannon than in love with him."

"The way I feel about you hasn't changed, Trace. Not in all this time."

Her eyebrows shot upward, her brow furrowing as her heart turned to lead.

Here she was trying to bare her soul to him, and he was telling her they were still just buddies. She felt like a first-class idiot. Everything was clear now. He'd kissed her the first time out of curiosity, nostalgia. The second time, he'd just been trying to comfort her.

She'd forgotten, hadn't she, about Miriam waiting for him back in Houston, that he had another life waiting for him? Surely he hadn't been waiting around for the past ten years, waiting to see her again. Hadn't he told her that first day he didn't expect to keep in contact with her?

She wriggled her hand free.

Rick realized too late she'd misinterpreted his

words. He was trying to tell her he'd always cared about her, forgetting she didn't know how he'd felt about her in the past. He could have kicked himself.

"Tracy," he said, just as the front door swung open and the man he'd been talking to earlier and his wife stepped out onto the porch.

"Nice breeze tonight," the woman commented.

Tracy's on-camera smile fell into place, and she exchanged a few pleasantries with her parents' guests before turning to run down the porch steps.

"I'll meet you there," she called to Rick, unable to endure the prospect of five minutes in the car with him.

As she sped off, she reflected how spoiled she was. She'd always gotten everything she wanted. Did she think Rick would love her just because she wanted that? Realizing just how much she did want that, she nearly burst into tears. He was the most honest, hardworking, good person she'd ever known. Was she acknowledging that too late?

She held back the threatening tears. She'd caved in to that weakness far too many times in the past few days. And she'd gotten where she was by being strong, not wimpy.

Rick must think her a total imbecile. She'd practically told him she was falling for him.

She realized she seldom revealed her true feelings to anyone anymore. It wasn't a wise practice in the world she moved within. She had walled her real self inside while everything on the outside was for show. The world watched her, and she didn't always like it.

Back in her parents' driveway, Rick was muttering curses as he hopped into the Bonneville. To think he'd come so close to possessing the one woman he'd always loved only to say something dumb enough to send her off like a scared rabbit. Maybe he didn't deserve to be happy.

All he wanted, he thought as he turned down the dusty road, was a chance to make Tracy happy. And oh, how he'd love trying!

If he could just stop mucking things up.

He pulled up in front of the white frame house, spotting Tracy's white Cutlass parked off to the side. She was sitting in the driver's side.

He got out of the car and walked over there cautiously.

''Tracy?'' he asked.

She extended the bouquet through the open window. ''I didn't want you to go in without these,'' she said.

He ignored the flowers, sidestepping them to reach the car door.

''You've got to let me explain what I meant back there,'' he urged.

She pressed a palm to her forehead. ''Not here and not now,'' she told him. ''I think what you said was pretty clear.'' She couldn't have stood to listen to him explain how her feelings were all tangled up with her memories of Shannon. She knew her own feelings, this time at least.

"It wasn't at all," he insisted, giving her a dark look. "Or you wouldn't have run off again. For Pete's sake, Tracy, stop running from me."

Her brow curved at his puzzling statement. She, running from him?

All at once Patsy was between them. "Come on, you two," she coaxed. "I've got steaks on the grill."

Food was the last thing on Tracy's mind, but she opened the car door and got out, aware of Rick's eyes on her. Something was very mixed up here.

As she turned to accompany Patsy to the house, she pressed the bunch of flowers into Rick's hand.

He said something under his breath, and she couldn't quite make it out.

She tossed him a questioning glance, then quickly turned to go.

He couldn't possibly have said what she thought he did, she reasoned. And she'd already embarrassed herself once by misunderstanding his actions. She wasn't going to make the same mistake twice.

Cilla cried and hugged Rick's neck when he presented her with the flowers.

She stepped back, wiping tears from her eyes.

"It's such a comfort to have you two here," she told him and Tracy.

Patsy brought Cilla a tissue, and everyone looked on awkwardly as she dried her face with it. "I promised myself I wasn't going to make a scene," she announced sheepishly, raising the rumpled tissue.

Tracy stepped forward and patted her shoulder. "We understand," she assured her.

Cilla nodded. "Thank you, dear."

Tracy wondered how Cilla held up as well as she did. Beneath that frail exterior was one tough trooper, she thought. Cilla's daughter, Shannon's mother, had died when Shannon was nine, and Shannon's father had abandoned him. She had raised her grandson only to lose him now.

"Let me find a vase for these, and we can all go out back," Cilla said, forcing a lighter tone. "Patsy's spent hours fixing a picnic for us."

As they ate, Tracy judged it was work well-done. Their meal was a feast of grilled steaks, potato salad, and corn on the cob, with lemonade and chocolate cake for dessert. Dining outdoors relaxed Tracy, and she ate more than she meant to. Finished, she sat back in a wooden chair and watched a cottony half-moon appear in the still-blue evening sky.

"This has been wonderful, Patsy," she said. "Thank you."

Rick was seated a few feet away from her. Although they'd scarcely spoken directly to each other throughout the evening, she was painfully aware of his presence, the intensity of his eyes scanning her when he thought she wasn't looking.

With a sweeping glance over the little gathering, Cilla determined everyone was finished eating.

"I have some news," she declared, tapping thin fingers against the picnic table.

All eyes turned to the elderly woman.

She looked at the ground before lifting her face to them once again. "I'm selling the house and leaving Cherry Cove."

Tracy's mouth dropped into a perfect O.

"Cilla, no!" she protested. "Where will you go?"

"I'm going back to Midland with Patsy." Her eyes drifted skyward.

"But you've always lived here."

Cilla shrugged. "There's nothing left for me here, child. I'm too old to run the store. My family's gone, and most of my friends have died. All that's left here are memories."

Tracy felt a lump rising in her throat.

"I don't know what Cherry Cove will be without you."

"Pretty much the same, I suppose." She forced a brave smile. "Maybe some of those yuppies who come down here from Houston on weekends will buy my house."

"Someone will buy it," Tracy conceded.

Cilla reached out and patted Tracy's hand. "Don't look so sad, Tracy. I've decided this is the only way I can bear to go on through my life. Change can be a very necessary thing. Memories can bring great happiness, but they can also be a huge burden. I need to be near my family. Remember that. I know I'm old-fashioned, but a family brings more joy in life than anything."

Tracy struggled to swallow the lump in her throat and ignored the heat of Rick's eyes on her. "When are you leaving?" she asked.

"After Sam arrives, I imagine. He'll be staying in the house while it's on the market. Patsy's helping me with the packing. After so many years, there are a lot of things to sort out."

"Is there anything I can do to help?" she asked.

Cilla shook her head. "What you and Rick are doing at the store right now is more than I could ever repay you for."

Tracy got up and refilled her lemonade glass. She wondered why she had stayed away from Cherry Cove so long, then returned expecting to find it intact, as she'd left it. Even a tiny place like this underwent constant change. Maybe she'd hoped to find in her past a key to what her life was all about now.

They sat talking quietly until long after dark. Tracy stared up at the brilliant stars sprinkled across the universe. Rick said little, and she attributed his silence to their earlier rift. As Cilla and Patsy talked of Midland, Patsy's family, and the city's activities for senior citizens, Tracy realized the older woman was looking forward to her new life. Even a person Cilla's age needed that, something to look forward to.

Finally she said good night, glancing at Rick as he made no move to follow her lead. Well, it wasn't her concern. He could come and go as he pleased.

Rick watched as she made her round of good-byes. He wanted a chance to settle their misunderstanding this afternoon, but he figured that would have to wait until tomorrow. Right now he had business to attend to with Cilla. Something unpleasant that was best to say and have it over with.

As they listened to Tracy's car door close and the engine start, Cilla sat back down, occupying the chair Tracy had vacated. Patsy busied herself moving dishes and leftovers inside.

"Now, what is it you want to tell me?" Cilla asked.

Rick gave her a lopsided smile. "Is there anything that escapes you, Cilla?"

"Not much," she admitted.

In the old days, when capturing an adult ear in his family's bustling household had been an impossible undertaking, Cilla had always made time to listen to him.

He rubbed a finger over his mustache. "It's not good," he reported.

"Just be straight with it, Rick."

He drummed his fingertips over the arm of the chair. "I went over the furniture store's books this afternoon. I'm not an accountant, but it's pretty obvious Shannon was having money problems."

Cilla was silent for a moment. Then she clicked her tongue in a "tisk" sound. "I anticipated this. He spent money like it was water, always had to put on a show for people, make them think he was something he wasn't. Have you seen his house?"

Rick gave her a vacant look. "Didn't he live here?"

She shook her head. "No, he hadn't for a long time. You know the house on the hill outside of town?"

Rick nodded.

"He bought it several years back."

"I don't know if the store's going to survive."

"I guess Sam and the lawyers will have to untangle all that. Money means little to me, Rick. I can get by. I just don't know why it was so all-important to Shannon. I suppose he was trying to make up for other things that were missing from his life. He always wanted so desperately for people to like him."

"They did like him, Cilla."

"But I don't think he ever realized they would

have anyway. Why did you wait until Tracy was gone to tell me this?"

"I didn't want to tarnish his image in front of her."

Cilla shook her head. "Even after all this time, you're still protecting her from the truth about him. When are you going to tell her how you feel about her?"

Caught off-guard, he froze, fidgeting with his collar.

Cilla continued. "I see it in your eyes every time you look at her. You're still in love with her, like you've always been. And if you were paying attention, you'd notice what's in her eyes when she looks at you. I have never seen two people so crazy about each other and too darn stubborn to admit it. Don't let her get away this time, Rick. You'll regret it the rest of your life."

"She thinks I'm her best friend."

"And who better to fall in love with?"

"I've tried to tell her, Cilla. But she turns and runs every time I do."

"Then you're not telling her the right way."

He gave her a sly grin. "Maybe you should talk to her."

"I think the effect would be more meaningful coming from you," she said. "But if that's what you want . . . "

"Don't you dare."

Rick mulled over Cilla's words all the way back to the Madisons' that night.

Maybe, he considered, she was right. Maybe he was taking the wrong approach. Things between him and Tracy had always been pretty straightforward. He'd never been very good at taking the roundabout approach. Now, he saw how it might work in his favor. Maybe Tracy assumed their relationship was the same because he was treating her the same way he always had.

He considered various methods of attempting to sweep her off her feet, dismissing most as absurd. He wanted to get her attention, not make her laugh.

He pulled the car up beside the stately Victorian house. The porchlight burned a welcome. He thought of Tracy, upstairs, probably asleep by now.

If he wanted to tell her he loved her, he couldn't just zap her with it out of the blue. He had to prepare her for it, he resolved.

Just as he began mounting the steps, through the corner of his eye he caught a movement out back. An animal or an intruder, he thought at first, then recognized Tracy's purposeful, rhythmic walk. She was headed for the barn.

Bewildered, he watched her march on intently. What was in the barn? There weren't any animals to tend to out there. The building was used mostly for storage.

Was she sleepwalking?

He didn't think so. She was dressed in cutoffs, tennis shoes without socks, and a T-shirt, not nightclothes.

Suppressing an impulse to call out to her, he followed her instead. He just wanted to make sure everything was all right.

Not calling out to her, he strode toward the barn, the dry ground crunching beneath the soles of his boots.

He watched the shadowy figure enter the barn, then followed close behind.

What in tarnation was she doing?

Nostalgically, he remembered the nights when he and she and Shannon had climbed out their bedroom windows to meet down by the creek. They passed those moon-drenched nights talking about their dreams, their futures, counting shooting stars and sipping canned colas Tracy sneaked out in her knapsack, and crunching potato chips and pretzels, which always tasted better in the open night air.

If they'd ever been caught, no one would have believed the simple innocence of their rendezvous. The escapes, as they'd referred to them, had been Shannon's idea. Rick had gone along because it was a dare, because he had known Tracy would be there.

Who would she be meeting now? he wondered, bristling at the prospect of her meeting anyone out here at night.

He stepped into the barn, blinking under a blaze

of electric lights. Squinting, he searched the expansive interior of the roomy outbuilding, seeing nothing but stacks of old junk—inner tubes, rakes, a rusty iron gate.

Just as he was about to call out to her, the shriek of a hyena came from above.

Astonished, he turned his head toward the loft.

"Yee-ha!" she hollered, swinging across the room on the end of a rope, her curls sticking straight out behind her as she flew. She released the rope, dropping none too daintily into a pile of hay.

Unaware of his presence, Tracy merrily turned a somersault in the pile of sweet-smelling straw.

Rick grinned broadly.

Brushing herself off, Tracy raised herself on one knee, looking toward the loft and contemplating another swing.

Suddenly her eyes caught movement near the doorway. Her face grew crimson, and she leaned back in alarm.

Rick's smile didn't fade. "Yee-ha!" he mocked her.

Her scowl turned to a smile. "What are you doing here?" she asked indignantly.

"I saw you coming this way. I thought something was wrong."

"Obviously, nothing is. You can leave now." She met his gaze. "If you want to."

He stepped closer. "What's the hay doing in here?"

"Mom and Dad got it for the hayride they're having for the guests Friday night."

Self-consciously, she plucked a piece of hay from her hair.

"May I?" he asked, gesturing toward the loft.

She beamed at him. "By all means."

She moved out of harm's way as he climbed the ladder. She tried not to admire so much the sure, steady way he moved.

She laughed wildly as he grabbed the rope and repeated her action, losing his hat as he sailed through the air.

"I've been wanting to do this ever since I got here," she confessed. "It's great. Takes your mind off everything else."

She raced for the wooden ladder.

Rick watched her as he moved out of the way. This was the Tracy he remembered, easy and free and a little wild. And he loved this part of her as much as he loved the serious young woman who had combed the store for a child's lost doll earlier.

They were both breathless by the time they'd had their fill of air travel. Rick sat down in the hay beside Tracy, who had just landed for the dozenth time.

He leaned back, admiring Tracy's relaxed, beautiful expression, the way her chest rose and fell as she lay back in happy exhaustion. Her face was flushed pink, her eyes wide and shining, her curls tousled, all mixed up with shards of straw.

She looked over at him, her mouth open slightly as she tried to stop laughing and catch her ragged breath.

She reached up to remove the straw from her hair, but he caught hold of her wrist.

"Don't," he said.

Her hand went limp.

Her laughter died as she met his gaze, her heart thundering. "Rick, it's not like it used to be. Every time you touch me . . . You can't keep doing this."

"Did you ever think that maybe I'm touching you because I don't want it to be the way it used to be?"

"But you said . . ."

"I said maybe you never understood the way I felt about you to begin with."

She raised her brows as his hands kneaded the soft skin on her neck. A warmth radiated through her.

"All this time?" she asked incredulously. "And you never said anything?"

He crossed one finger over her lips to silence her.

"It's like touching velvet," he whispered, his voice husky as his fingers worked her muscles into butter.

Tracy closed her eyes, losing all sense except the brush of his skin and the smell of hay. She felt his breath in wisps on her face, the rise and fall of his chest as he eased her back on the hay.

Her eyes fluttered open, and content at the sight of his smile as his face hovered over hers, she closed them again, letting his kiss cover her like a quilt in winter.

Rick kissed her leisurely, relishing the softness of her skin against the prickly hay.

Tracy returned the gesture easily, gliding through a universe of powerful currents that startled her as they gradually intensified. Everything in her life had somehow been building toward this moment. The pressure of Rick's lips against hers felt almost too right.

After a long moment, he drew back, sitting up and drawing in a long breath. He raked a hand through his hair.

Tracy watched him for several seconds. She closed her eyes and sank back in the hay, dwelling on what just happened and trying to let logic catch up to her emotions. Her lingering dizziness reminded her of stepping off an amusement-park ride. The annoying sensations didn't stop you from wanting to get right back on again.

"You can run in the house if you want to," Rick offered generously.

She sat up beside him. "I don't guess it would do much good. We'd just have to go through all this again tomorrow."

He smiled at the irony. "Promise?"

She threw a handful of straw at him.

She propped an elbow on one knee, resting her chin. "I think what happened—"

"Was the most natural thing in the world," he finished.

Her eyes swerved to meet his.

She hugged her knees. "Maybe it was," she admitted. "But I wonder whether it's fair to either of us," she added. "I think at this point in my life I really need somebody. And I've always felt secure with you. You accuse me of running from you, but wouldn't it be worse to run to you just because the world's a little out of sync right now?"

"Believe it or not, I have no intention of pushing you into something you're not ready for." Rick looked down at his boots, meaning what he'd said. Nothing regarding the way he felt about her was casual, and he didn't want their relationship to be that way. He didn't want her to come to him to ease old wounds. He wanted to bring something new and wonderful into their lives, to start over.

She smiled gorgeously, rising up to plant a kiss on his lips.

"Good night, Rick," she said, a funny expression crossing her face as she looked at him.

Rick flipped a piece of straw in the air as he watched her go. He had made some headway, after all, he thought. She hadn't run off this time. But regardless, here he was, alone and wanting to win her more than ever. He had done it to himself, he noted.

As he left the barn, he discovered a misty rain had begun to fall.

He shook his head. He was crazy to have stayed here in Cherry Cove. After all, if Tracy cared about him the way he always had about her, wouldn't she have known it years ago?

It was true, what they say. You can never go back.

Chapter Six

"I couldn't believe it when I called your parents' house and was given the phone number for a furniture store."

Tracy smiled slightly at the familiar sound of her producer's voice over the phone line, reminding her of the life she'd left behind back in Dallas. She tapped a pencil on the desktop.

"It's a long story, Hank. I'm helping out a friend for a few days."

"Make sure that's all it is. I need you back here. Your replacement is doing an abysmal job."

"I'm sure he's not that bad. I might remind you it was your idea I take a vacation."

"To rest, Trace. I might remind you the term vacation conjures up images of lying on beaches, hiking in the woods, long leisurely meals. Not, to most, working in a furniture store.''

She wrinkled her nose, watching Rick pacing on the opposite end of the showroom floor. Was he, too, becoming restless, anxious to return to the world where he belonged?

''This is only for a day or two more, until the owner arrives. It's a long story.''

''Well, do something for yourself. How did it go with the funeral and all?''

''I'm handling it, thanks.''

Several minutes of shop talk followed. Tracy realized how much she missed her fast-paced schedule. She hated the idea that the weatherman was filling in on her show. Rick had been right—she could never stay in Cherry Cove. But she couldn't leave now because of her commitment to Cilla and because she had to know where she and Rick stood with each other.

He had said last night he'd always cared about her. She was still trying to comprehend that. If it was true, why had he never told her?

She drew a line across the desk with the pencil's eraser.

Hank's tone grew serious. ''You've got another week,'' he decreed. ''Have some fun. Although I can't imagine what you'll do to accomplish that in Cherry Cove.''

"There's a hayride Friday night," she told him with a laugh.

"With a barn raising afterward?" he asked.

"Sure. Just before the quilting bee, taffy pull, and gunfight."

"Well, don't overexcite yourself. See you in a week."

Tracy gently replaced the receiver. Was there room in her life for anything but her work? she wondered. Yet what kind of life was it with nothing else in it? She remembered Cilla's advice about family being all-important. But Cilla was from another generation. Women from her era centered their lives around their family, or they had nothing—no challenging career—just long lonely hours.

"Everything okay?"

She looked up to see Rick standing close by. The sight of his fine, handsome face struck a chord in her heart. She knew what she wanted out of life, but how much better it would be to come home at night and see that face.

"Sure," she answered, remembering how his kiss, his touch had set her heart racing last night. Suppose they fell in love, she considered. How much would she have to give up? Everything? Was she willing to give up anything?

"I thought maybe you'd gotten some bad news."

She shook her head. "Nothing like that. I was just thinking."

He looked puzzled as he reached in the pocket of his jeans, producing a penny and planting it on the desktop.

A slow smile rose to her lips.

"I was thinking about this store," she confessed. "I know it meant something to Shannon, but I don't think I would find much satisfaction in selling furniture one day, then coming back just to sell furniture again the next."

Rick nodded. "Actually, Shannon was pretty ingenious to establish a business this big in Cherry Cove. He may have saved the town from extinction and in the process saved the smaller businesses—your parents' business, for example."

"People come to my parents' to get away from it all, because this town is quaint and charming. Cherry Cove is a kind of refuge, not much like the real world."

Rick flashed a crooked smile. "You once described this place as stifling and monotonous."

She shrugged. "I'd forgotten. All that was a lifetime ago. My outlook has changed."

"And we're different people with different lives now."

Her eyes met his for an instant. Did either of them have room in their lives for the other? Or were the sparks between them some temporary madness that coincided with a certain phase of the moon and would vanish when their time here together was over?

The prospect frightened her. She had found something here she dreaded losing.

He swung his head from side to side, bending his elbow awkwardly to massage the back of his neck. "Stiff neck," he explained.

"Maybe you've been spending too many hours poring over Shannon's books," she observed.

"Somebody's got to look out for Cilla."

She rose from her chair, gesturing with an open palm for him to sit down.

He eyed her skeptically.

"Go on," she ordered. "I won't hurt you."

Resigned, he dropped his lanky frame into the chair.

"Who would suspect," she said, as she began kneading the taut muscles in his shoulders, "that a rough, tough bronco rider would get cramps from sitting over a desk?"

"That feels great," he admitted, ignoring her sarcasm. Relaxing, he felt the crispness of her blouse against the back of his head, the warmth radiating from beneath it. He closed his eyes. "Where did you learn how to do this?"

"In college. Those cramming sessions were rough."

"And who helped you through them?" he inquired.

"A friend," she answered, swiftly changing the subject. "What did you find in the books?"

"Not much," he said evasively.

"You forget I started out as a reporter. Not much of what? Income?"

"There was plenty of income. But most of it is gone, Cilla's share as well as Shannon's. He must have believed he'd have plenty of time to earn it back."

"Maybe Sam will be a financial genius."

"A magician is more what's needed."

Tracy caressed the toughened skin on the back of his neck. She liked feeling him relax beneath her hands.

"Whatever he is," she said with a sigh, "I wish he'd hurry and arrive. Running a store every day is very confining."

"Confining," he noted. "That's it!"

"That's what?" she asked, stepping back.

He turned to her. "That's the term you always used for Cherry Cove."

"You remember so much."

"You forget so much."

His eyes held hers again.

Tracy felt the heat rising in her cheeks. "Did you mean what you said in the barn last night?"

"I said a lot of things in the barn last night."

"About the way you'd always felt."

"Yes."

"I just can't imagine why you never said anything."

"I guess I envisioned being there to pick up the pieces when you and Shannon broke up for good. Of course, it didn't work out that way."

"We were so young."

"And foolish," he added. "Look, why don't you go home early? I'll pick up a movie and we can watch it later."

"I'd feel like I was abandoning you."

He lowered his voice. "George and Mrs. Harding are running the place. There's no point in both of us being cooped up here."

Tracy considered. "All right. But I'll pay you back in the morning. You can take some time off while I come down here."

"Fair enough," he agreed, rising from the chair. "Now scat before I change my mind."

After retrieving her pocketbook from the desk drawer, she raised up on tiptoe to plant a kiss on his lips.

"Keep doing that," he warned, his firm hands cradling her elbows, "and I won't let you go."

Rebelliously, she gave him a second kiss before leaving. As she marched off, he wondered if she would have dared if she knew the overpowering ache in his chest she had triggered.

But she would be his for the evening at least. He was going to have to make the most of it.

Suddenly Rick realized the danger of their tentative relationship. If he left Cherry Cove without her this time, she'd be lost to him forever.

Carrying a gigantic bowl of popcorn under one arm, Tracy entered the back rec room and saw Rick had already popped a videocassette into the VCR.

"So, what are we watching first?" she asked. Unable to decide, she'd rented three—a thriller, a Western, and a comedy.

"The funny stuff," he replied, turning and holding her with his eyes. She looked different somehow this evening, her curls falling softly against the contours of her face, her skin rosy and glowing.

"You look nice."

Caught off-guard, she warmed under his praise. He looked pretty appealing himself, his dark hair combed back from his forehead. "Thank you," she said, smiling up at him.

She set the heavy ceramic bowl on an end table, then got comfortable on one end of the sofa. Rick sat beside her. He smelled the familiar scent of her light perfume, the jasmine and oranges, and realized there was nowhere else in the world he'd rather be right now.

He hated the prospect of her going back on her own to Dallas. And he dreaded the thought of returning to Houston alone. Whatever it took, he couldn't just let her slip away this time.

Leaning back, he wound an arm around her shoulders. She moved closer, and he savored the feel of her delicate frame against him.

The movie played, and they watched in comfortable silence. It was a good film, and soon they were laughing together over it.

Rick realized they had finally relaxed with each other. But would this cozy feeling last without the diversion of the movie?

Suddenly a flash of lightning cut through darkness beyond the sliding-glass doors that looked out over the back porch and the woods. Thunder rumbled in the distance.

Tracy scooted closer to Rick. "It's going to storm," she noted.

"Well, at least we're inside," he replied. "And neither of us is afraid of a storm."

"I like them," she admitted, smoothing her hair back. "The earth always smells so sweet afterward. That's something I miss about living in the city."

She settled back, resting her head against his chest.

Concentrating on the movie, she blocked out the thunder and lightning, the sudden beating of rain on the roof.

In the midst of a car chase, the machine whirled to halt, and Tracy discovered they were in total darkness.

"The electricity's out," she said.

He tightened his grip on her shoulder. "Then we'll just stay here until it comes back on," he suggested.

She looked up sidewise at him. "All right," she agreed, settling back against his chest and watching the flashes of lightning through the window.

Finally she broke the silence. "My producer called today," she told him.

Rick felt a tightening in his chest. She'd be going back soon. Maybe he was wrong to rush her, but maybe he didn't have all that much time.

"And?" he asked quietly.

"He gave me another week." Relief rushed through Rick's veins.

"That was good of him."

"Surely Shannon's cousin will be here by then."

"It doesn't matter. I don't think anyone could save that store."

Her eyes narrowed with concern. "Are you sure?"

"I wouldn't place any bets on it. Shannon just spent too much money." Thinking of Cilla, Rick gritted his teeth. "Didn't he ever think of how his actions affected anyone else?"

Her answer surprised him. "No," she said. "He never did. Shannon needed people but he didn't know how to give back. That's why he kept us close."

Knowing what this assessment had cost her, Rick pulled her closer to him.

Tracy closed her eyes, listening to the intrusive sounds of thunder and rain. Beneath it all, she could hear Rick's heartbeat.

And suddenly she knew from her soul that it had been Rick she'd missed all these long years. It had always been Rick she loved. Shannon's charm had just drawn her youthful attention. Somehow, the two had gotten mixed up in her emotions.

Until now.

Raising her head, she looked up at Rick, the lines of his face shadowy in the darkness.

"It was you," she said with awe. "It was you all along."

Rick's chest swelled as her soft words fell on his ears.

"I've always loved you, Trace," he said. "Always."

His lips pressed down on hers, and Tracy welcomed the swirling joy that spiraled through her. They'd both made some mistakes, but now, somehow, everything would work out.

She raised one small hand to caress the back of his head, raking her fingers through his thick hair. The scent of him filled her senses, and she wanted this moment to stay frozen in time forever.

His name played over and over again in her head, and then she realized someone was calling it. Her mother.

She broke away from him, and Rick cleared his throat. "We're in here," he called.

Tracy rose and found her mother standing in the doorway with a flashlight.

"You have a phone call, Rick. Someone from your company. He said it was important."

Rick grumbled inwardly. Nothing could be more important than what had just happened.

He groped his way toward the kitchen, finding the flashlight beam Mrs. Madison shined to guide the way of little use.

Finally he was in the kitchen and picked up the receiver.

"What?" he asked, his mind on Tracy back in the other room.

But the voice on the other end said something that caught his immediate attention.

"All right," he said in a grave tone and hung up.

He turned soberly, startled to see Tracy instead of Mrs. Madison standing a few feet away.

"What is it?" she asked.

"There's been a fire at one of the construction sites. I've got to go back to Houston."

Tracy gasped. "No, Rick, not so soon."

"I'll be back," he promised. "I'll be back before you leave for Dallas."

Tracy chewed her lip. There was so little time, and they'd just found each other. But his company needed him, and she had no right to make demands.

"I've got to go upstairs and pack a few things," he said. "Where did your mother disappear to? Do you think she'd have another flashlight I could borrow?"

"You're going tonight?" she asked.

"I have to leave now."

She fished under the sink to produce an ancient-looking flashlight. After she shook it a couple of times, it produced a faint beam of light.

"Just shake it if it goes out," she advised, handing it to him.

"Thanks," he said, his eyes lingering on her silhouette. Just his luck to have to leave when they'd started working things out.

Tracy stayed alone in the darkened kitchen as he navigated the staircase.

His leaving was just another reminder of how far apart their lives had grown. With a deep sigh, she knew she had to stay and keep the store open until Sam arrived. No matter what the business's future, she had promised Cilla.

She sat at the small table and propped her chin on one elbow until she heard Rick's footsteps on the stairs. She met him in the hall.

"I'll walk out to the car with you," she offered, hating the sight of the bag in his hand.

"Thanks," he said. "But I don't want you to get wet on my account."

She shook her head. "I think it's stopped raining."

He nodded, taking hold of her hand with his free one.

"We've got a lot of talking to do," he said, leading her across the muddy yard. "I'll be back as soon as I can."

She nodded. "I'll be here, Rick," she assured him.

He opened his car door and tossed the bag in the backseat.

Turning to her, he took both of her hands in his.

"This is a lousy time for a fire," he noted.

She laughed lightly. "I don't think there's a good time for something like that. Will this hurt your business?"

He shook his head. "It will set us back on meeting the contract deadline, but we'll manage. Fortunately, no one was hurt."

"Rick . . . "

He leaned down and kissed her. She closed her eyes, memorizing the taste and touch of his lips against her skin in the damp night air.

As they drew apart, his eyes swept over her, as if he, too, were storing memories.

"I'll be back in a few days," he repeated.

Tracy believed him, yet she wondered why there was a prickling fear in her heart that he wouldn't come back to her, that his leaving now would change everything.

Rick took a last, hard look at her as he climbed into the car. He had so much to say to her. Yet it was important enough that it would have to keep.

She watched him drive away, ignoring the rain that had kicked up again and was pelting her in fat, cold drops.

No matter what, Rick owned her heart. He always had and always would.

Chapter Seven

As Tracy was dressing early the next morning, she heard the phone ringing downstairs. Immediately, her thoughts flew to Rick. Quickly, she pulled on her jeans and bolted down the stairs.

"Hello?" she said breathlessly, disappointment trickling through her as a stranger's voice responded.

She ran one hand across her unruly mass of curls as she listened, and a new reality set in.

Finally she fumbled for a notepad and paper, jotting down a name, address, and phone number.

When the conversation ended, she stood staring at the telephone.

"Something wrong?" her mother asked.

Tracy shifted her glance from the phone to her

mother and back again. Then she broke into a tentative grin.

"I've been asked to visit New York for an interview with the network."

"I thought you were going to quit and stay here in Cherry Cove," her mother teased.

"No way," Tracy assured her. "I was just upset. Mom, I've been waiting all my life for that phone call—" She broke off her sentence as she caught the glint in her mother's eye and realized she didn't have to explain all this.

With her sweeping gesture, she hugged her mother and, mindful of the guests still asleep upstairs, suppressed a whoop.

"I am so proud of you," Alice Madison said.

"I know, Mom. Thanks."

Joy coursed through Tracy's heart. Yet a lingering hollowness nagged her. She only wished Rick were here so she could share this with him.

Her smile fell. "They might not like me," she speculated.

Alice laughed. "They'll like you. Stop worrying."

Tracy sighed. "I'd better finish dressing so I can get to the furniture store."

"We'll celebrate later," Alice assured her.

Tracy beamed. "Don't go to any trouble, Mom." Sharing the news with Rick was the only celebration she needed. But she didn't know how to contact him. Besides, she didn't want to bother him when he had a business problem to tend to.

There would be time enough to tell him when he got back. She hoped. The trip to New York would require leaving a few days before she was due back at work.

She went back upstairs and finished dressing, thoughts of Rick intruding on what should have been unrestrained happiness. Her new job would take her even farther away from him. And even sooner.

Tracy managed to keep busy most of the day. In the afternoon, the sky grew overcast, making the store's interior dark and gloomy.

While things were quiet, she poured a cup of coffee and retreated to Shannon's office, opening the bulky ledger and trying to decipher the numbers. But they made little sense to her.

"Excuse me," a voice drifted in from the showroom.

Open-mouthed, she looked up, embarrassed that a customer had entered the store without her noticing. Where was Mrs. Harding?

Her eyes flared dramatically at the sight of the young man in jeans, running shoes, and a polo shirt. Blood rushed to her head.

For a second she thought she was seeing a ghost.

He approached her rapidly, his expression ruled by concern.

She looked up, aware of a steadying hand on her shoulder.

"You're Sam," she ventured, struggling to smile.

"Yes, I am. Are you all right? You went so pale, I thought you were going to faint."

She waved off his suggestion. "I'm not the fainting type," she insisted. "It's just that you look so much like your cousin. For a moment . . ."

"Ah. I'm sorry I scared you. It never crossed my mind that I resembled Shannon that closely."

"Well, now that I see you up close, I realize you don't. It's just that I was going over the books and thinking about Shannon when I first saw you." She broke off her rambling explanation. "You'll have to excuse me. This has been a very emotional time."

He nodded, removing his hand now that he was convinced she was all right. He offered a handshake. "You must be Tracy." My grandmother said I'd find you here."

He walked to a chair in front of the desk. His gait was measured and even, just like Shannon's, she reflected.

She realized she was staring. "Your grandmother never mentioned how much you and Shannon favored each other."

He shrugged. "A slight family resemblance. Actually, Shannon and I only met a few times through the years. I'm sorry I missed his funeral, though."

"It was pretty rough on Cilla."

"I'm glad she's coming back to stay with my mom." His glance swept over the showroom. "Sorry it took me so long to get here, but I had job responsibilities to untangle. I don't know what I'm going to do with this place."

She nodded toward the ledger. "I hate to tell you this after you've come all this way, but Rick says it's in pretty bad shape."

His face went blank momentarily.

"Oh, Shannon's other friend," he said. "Well, I'm an accountant, so maybe I can figure out whether it's salvageable."

"I hope it is," she agreed. "The store means a lot to the town."

He leaned forward, inspecting the lines of figures upside down. Tracy had the oddest sensation of Shannon's shadow crossing over her. She knew this was Sam, a stranger, and yet she felt as though she'd known him for a long time.

"It's like Greek to me," she admitted.

He smiled easily. "Thank heaven for that. People like you keep me in business. Also I understand you're about to become a famous television star, so you may be requiring my services."

"How . . . ?" She raised a hand to her temple. "Oh, my mother. She should go to work for one of the wire services. And I've only got an interview, so I don't think I should be counting my money just yet."

"She's obviously very happy for you. As she has a right to be."

Tracy straightened the hem of her blouse. "Let me find George and Mrs. Harding and introduce you. They're actually the ones who have been keeping this place going. And Rick. But he's not here. He had to go back to Houston."

"I can't tell you how much I appreciate your keeping this place open. I know it's well out of your line of work."

"I'd do just about anything for Cilla," she said. "Besides, now I have something else to tack on to my résumé in case my television career falls through."

"Slim chance of that, I'd guess," he said, following her through the maze of furniture. "But I'm granting you your freedom so you can enjoy the last few days of your vacation."

She turned to him. "Is there anything about me that my mother didn't tell you?" she asked.

"Not much, I think. You were in love with my cousin once."

She colored. "When we were teenagers."

"When you were teenagers," he added.

"You're at an unfair advantage, knowing so much about me when I scarcely know a thing about you."

"Touché. Maybe you should have a cup of coffee with my mother."

She laughed.

"Then again, maybe you'd better not. She exaggerates a little."

"I guess she's just proud of you."

"I know it's kind of late in the day, but I haven't had any lunch, and my stomach is rumbling furiously. Can we go get a hamburger? You can fill me in on the store and the town, and I'll divulge my mysterious background."

"Fair enough," Tracy agreed.

She knew she should have been relieved to be free of the store, but now that Sam was here, she was a little reluctant to let go of it. While she'd needed these days back in Cherry Cove to set her past in perspective, his presence was proof they were numbered.

Life never goes backward, she reflected. Any journey into the past is just an illusion produced by old memories. She thought of the new job awaiting her, and she thought of Rick. Was there any way she could have both in her life?

Absently, she bit her lip. If she had to choose between the two, which would she take?

She'd put long hours into her television career, no great sacrifice, really, because time just flowed for her when she was in the studio. The job was so much a part of her, she wondered what she would be without it.

But now that she'd found Rick again, could she

go back to her solitary life without missing him every minute, wondering what might have been?

Perhaps, she thought, it would be easier on everyone if she went back to Dallas early, before Rick returned.

"Where could Tracy be?" Alice Madison asked anxiously as her husband paced to the front window for the fifteenth time in as many minutes.

"She left the store hours ago," Sam said. "I could get in my car and go look for her."

Alice looked over the small congregation of guests, then straightened the line of dishes in the buffet she'd set out on the dining-room table. "You've been traveling all morning, Sam. But thank you, anyway."

"She knows her way home," Matt Madison put in. In his boots, jeans, and chambray shirt, he looked slightly out of place in his own home. A man of average height, he was squarely built and sported a mass of graying, curly hair.

Alice cast him a distracted glance. "But it's not like her to be late for a party."

"I thought this was a surprise party!" Sam exclaimed.

Tracy's father chuckled.

"Tracy knows her mother too well to expect she'd let an occasion like this pass without fanfare."

Cilla, seated on one side of the living room beside

Mrs. Harding, cleared her throat. "She's got a lot on her mind these days. I'm sure she'll be here in good time."

As darkness fell outside, Alice turned on the lamps. They glowed invitingly as everyone forced conversation and awaited the arrival of the guest of honor.

Tracy spotted squares of light shining through the window as she drove up. Counting the number of cars parked outside, she realized what was going on. She'd forgotten the celebration her mom had promised earlier.

Now she was late for her own party.

Driving for hours, mulling over her problems, she'd lost track of time.

Although she definitely was not in a party mood, she shook her curls, took a deep breath, and forced a smile in place before getting out of the car.

Rick's coming back, now that would be something to celebrate. But his car was not among those parked in the yard.

She walked inside to a barrage of good wishes and concerned inquiries.

"You said you wouldn't do this," she accused her mother.

"I couldn't help myself," she replied.

Tracy nodded. Her mother was a very giving person. She wished she were more like her.

Somehow Alice had managed to keep the food

hot, and Tracy found she had more of an appetite than she'd imagined. Dessert was a huge cake topped with a crude version of the network logo painted in colored icing.

As it was placed in front of her, Tracy laughed with delight.

Once it was cut, Alice invited the few guests upstairs to come down and join them for cake and coffee.

As the party progressed, Tracy slipped away from the crowd into the kitchen. She eyed the telephone and considered calling Rick. His voice would have been a welcome sound.

But the things she had to say to him were too important to be said over the phone. They were meant to be said face to face.

"You're missing your party," a voice accused from the doorway.

She looked up and saw Sam standing there.

She flushed. "My mother goes overboard sometimes."

"She's proud of you," he said, slipping into the kitchen chair opposite her.

"I know. It's just a little overwhelming at times."

"Your mom's great. I just got to town this morning, and she's already made me feel like part of the family."

Tracy smiled. "My mom always wanted a big family. When she couldn't have one, she just reached out to take care of friends, the guests here. When we were teenagers, Rick and Shannon used to spend hours in this kitchen talking to her. She's a good listener."

Sam traced the edge of the table with his fingertip. "It makes me sorry I'm not going to be able to stay here long."

Her eyebrows arched as she looked over at him. "And the store?"

He shook his head. "From what I saw this afternoon, it would be too risky to try to keep it open. I don't want my grandmother burdened by debts."

Tracy nodded gravely. "I wish Shannon had planned better."

"I'm sure he thought he had all the time he needed to straighten things out."

"And then he didn't. What about Mrs. Harding and George?"

Sam shrugged helplessly. "Mrs. Harding's pretty much retired, and George is young and hardworking enough he shouldn't have a problem finding something else."

"It will be bad for the town, losing the store. But I realize you don't have any choice."

"I have a few ideas I'm going to look into. As popular as the location has become, a chain might be willing to come in."

Tracy brightened. "You're a pretty smart guy, Sam."

"I take that as high praise coming from you," he replied. "But actually, I doubt Cilla would allow me to close the store if she thought it was going to destroy the town's economy. She'd rather bear the losses herself."

"Just like Cilla," Tracy agreed. "And of course you can't let her do that."

"No," Sam concluded with a heavy sigh. "But I will be here a few weeks to straighten things out."

"Just call if you need any help. Now that I know the furniture business inside out," she joked.

"You can tell me what there is to do around here."

Tracy pondered his request. Then she looked up. "You like to fish?"

"As a matter of fact, I do."

"Okay, we can go fishing sometime before you leave."

"It's a deal. So what are you going to do with your first day of freedom?"

She shrugged. "Sleep in, I suppose. Maybe I'll drive to Houston."

He rubbed his jaw. "Your friend doesn't know yet about the call from the network?"

"No, he doesn't know." She looked up at him. "He's more than a friend, actually."

"I got that impression."

She clasped one hand to her forehead. "I'd forgotten your long talk with Mom."

"I think she was trying to warn me away from you."

"How embarrassing. I have to apologize."

He held up one hand. "Not necessary," he insisted. "I can't wait to meet Rick. And I might be asking you out right now if I weren't planning to be married in the fall."

She broke into a smile. "Congratulations," she said. "Do you have a photograph of her?"

He fished in his pocket for his wallet. "It just so happens, I do."

The picture of the young woman with long, dark hair reminded Tracy of Miriam, and she immediately thought of Rick in Houston. But she was being foolish. Hadn't Rick told her he had always loved her?

But what now?

She realized she was gaping at the photograph.

"She's gorgeous," she said.

"And your mind is somewhere else," he observed.

She shook her head. "I don't mean to be rude. It's just been a long day. I think I'll start picking up some of the dishes."

"Can I help?" he asked.

"Guests never help here. House rules," she insisted.

Reluctantly, he drifted back into the living room as she began rinsing dishes in the sink. Several minutes later her mother was by her side, stacking platters on the counter.

"It was a nice party, Mom," she said. "Thanks."

"Where did you run off to? Everyone was worried about you."

Tracy watched steam waft from the chrome sink. "I was just driving around. Thinking."

"Come to any conclusions?"

"None."

"You're not having second thoughts about the job, are you?"

"No. I know I want it as much as I've ever wanted anything. I just wish I knew what Rick would think about it."

"Well, he'll be delighted for you. You know that."

"I love him, Mom."

Alice emitted a surprised gasp.

"So you're wondering if you'll have to choose between the two?"

"It's a long way from New York to Houston."

Alice's brow creased as she studied her daughter's face. "Has he asked you to marry him?"

"No," she answered quietly. "I guess that makes it easier, doesn't it?"

"Give it time," Alice advised, wiping her hands on a dishcloth.

Tracy's glance shot up to meet hers. "That's just what I haven't got very much of."

Alice shut the dishwasher door and sank into one of the chairs beside the table. "Nobody wants to see you and Rick together as much as I do. But you're both still shaken over Shannon's death, and what you've found together is still brand-new."

"Mom, I've known Rick forever."

"But you were thinking of him in a different way. You've only just now discovered you love him, and you've got to give that time. You can't let everything rest on a few days."

Tracy folded the dishrag over the sink divider and joined her mother at the table.

"I'm just afraid that if I leave, I'll lose him."

"If that's true, you would have lost him eventually anyway. If the two of you are meant to be together, you will be."

Tracy sighed. "I don't want to be alone with a lot of regrets."

"Speaking of regrets, how will you feel if you give up a chance at something you've been working toward all these years? Would you have anything left to offer?"

"Why can't this be easy?" Tracy wailed.

Alice laughed lightly. "Nothing worth having comes easily. I'm exhausted, and breakfasttime comes early around here."

"Good night, Mom."

"Good night, dear. Get some rest."

Tracy watched her mother disappear toward the stairway before she got up and turned out the lights.

She supposed there was no point in traveling to Houston tomorrow. She wouldn't know what to tell Rick when she got there.

Chapter Eight

Friday evening just after dark, Rick parked his car around the side of the old Victorian house, noticing several others already there. Business must be good for the Madisons this weekend, he noted.

He got out of the car, balancing a cardboard pizza box. Unpacking the trunk could wait until later, he resolved. For now, all he wanted to do was see Tracy.

She'd been on his mind the whole time he was straightening out the mess in Houston. So many times, he'd nearly reached for the phone and called her. But always, he'd held back.

He didn't see how he could talk to her without telling her what was on his mind. And he certainly didn't want to ask her to be his wife via long-distance.

The more he thought about it, the more right it felt. He'd taken his business far enough that he wasn't tied to Houston full-time. Somehow it could work. While he could ask her to share her life with him, he couldn't ask her to give up a dream that had put a light in her eyes since she was a teenager.

He sauntered up the porch steps and into the house, surprised to find no one there.

"Hello?" he called out, puzzled.

No answer came.

Confused, he went back outside. Gazing across the field, he spotted the red glow of a fire through the darkness. Of course, he'd forgotten the hayride.

Still carrying the pizza, he headed off across the field. An occasional firefly flickered in his path. He heard the sound of distant voices, felt hard earth and dry grass beneath his boots.

Cherry Cove would always be home to him, he reflected. It was a strange kind of place that called him back even though he knew he could never stay. He regretted having avoided it for so long. But there had been no point in coming back after Tracy had left.

Crossing the field took longer than he'd anticipated. As he neared the campfire, he made out the outline of a hay wagon parked some distance away from the circle of people perched on stools around the fire.

Their faces were indistinguishable, but he searched for the familiar mop of blond curls.

Before he saw it, he heard his name being called.

One of the stools was quickly abandoned, and Tracy barreled across the rocky terrain toward him.

She halted in front of him, somewhat breathless and offering an unrestrained smile.

"I thought you were never coming back," she said, brushing stray curls from her forehead.

She was dressed simply, in a pair of jeans and a white shirt and loafers, but she looked better than ever to him. He detected the faint scent of oranges and jasmine drifting in the night air, and he wanted to scoop her into his arms and never let go.

But he still held the pizza box tilted in his arms, abandoning any hope of embracing her now as he grew aware they had an audience. He would have to wait longer still before they were alone together.

"I told you I'd be back," he said evenly.

So many times while he was gone, he'd wondered if that last night here had been a dream, if he'd come back to find everything had changed.

"I missed you," she said softly, her voice a quiet melody.

His eyes probed hers. And he knew what he had found here was very real.

Remembering the group around the fire, he held

back his emotions, afraid to unleash them here in front of everybody.

He held out the box. "I brought you a pizza," he told her, thinking now a bouquet of roses might have been more appropriate. Why hadn't he thought of that? How many guys proposed over pepperoni? "I guess I should have stashed it in the refrigerator."

She accepted the box from him, aware of a tingling in her arms as they brushed his. How could she ever have considered leaving without seeing him again? she wondered.

"Thanks," she said, touched that he'd remembered her fondness for pizza. "I'll put it up on the tractor until we're ready to go."

Rick did a double take as Shannon's image appeared over her shoulder.

Catching his shocked expression, Tracy turned to see Sam standing behind her. And she understood.

"This is Shannon's cousin, Sam," she said. "Sam, this is Rick."

Sam enthusiastically extended one hand. "You're the man I've been waiting to talk to," he said.

Rick looked at him blankly.

"About the furniture store," Shannon explained.

Rick's expression tightened. "Of course, the store. I'm no expert, but it's not good news," he said.

"I know," Sam agreed. "And some people might consider me an expert."

As reluctant as she was to leave Rick's side, Tracy stepped away to put up the pizza box, leaving him and Sam to discuss the store. She didn't understand the financial end of the business and wouldn't pretend to.

She returned alone to the fire, joining the group of her parents' guests and several of the townspeople. From the fireside, she watched Rick, standing straight and tall. A wave of admiration crossed over her. Solid, strong, steady, and with a bigger heart than he let on, that was how he'd always been.

And maybe it was the simple good things in life that don't call out for attention that were always overlooked, she reflected. She'd aimed for bright stars, but now that they were almost within reach, it was Rick's serene intensity she yearned for.

A rustling beside her announced Rick's presence as he occupied a vacant stool.

Her face hot from the flames, she cast him a look that conveyed all the tender words she couldn't say right now. And the look he gave her in return flooded her heart with delight.

He captured her small hand in his, and the momentary connection made her feel happy and secure.

Sam, sitting on Rick's other side, was passing them long sticks and marshmallows.

Tracy accepted hers and gleefully speared the sugary confection onto the pointed end of the stick her dad had whittled clean of bark earlier in the day.

"I haven't done this in years," she admitted.

Rick caught her glance, his features illuminated by the flickering firelight.

Her mouth fell open as she remembered. The night before his family moved away, she and Rick and Shannon had come out here and built a fire. They had toasted marshmallows that night between promises of how they'd always be friends, no matter what circumstances life dealt them.

It was the last time she'd seen Rick until after Shannon's funeral. Until now.

Was the past repeating itself? Would they part with more promises that neither would keep? Her heart lurched at the thought. Even if she attained fame and fortune, her life would be unbearably empty without Rick.

Somehow she would work that part of her life out, even if it meant taking a lesser job to be closer to him. She was willing to compromise. All she needed was a word from him.

She held her stick over the fire. The marshmallow immediately burst into flames. She jerked the stick back, watching helplessly as the marshmallow burned.

Laughing, Rick placed a hand on the stick and turned it up, blowing out the blazing candy. It was still smoking as he offered the charred remnant to her.

"You're supposed to hold it over the embers, so

this won't happen,'' he advised. His face was inches from hers, and she longed to reach out and touch his clean-shaven cheek.

He removed his stick, displaying a puffy, lightly browned marshmallow. ''Here, you can have this one.''

She shook her head stubbornly. ''No, that's yours. I'll eat this one.''

''Suit yourself,'' he conceded.

She pulled off the charred coating with her fingertips.

Rick watched her with amusement. He wanted to be alone with her, to kiss her and tell her how much he loved her, that he wanted to spend the rest of his life loving her as he'd never been free to do before.

Someone had rigged up a stereo, and the twang of country music echoed through the night. The crowd began to mingle, and Rick found himself dragged off to see an old friend from high school he hadn't recognized earlier.

''I'm glad someone from our class turned out to be successful,'' Brad, a tall, young man with prematurely graying hair, told him.

Rick shrugged as he looked anxiously around for Tracy. ''It's just a little construction company. Nothing to get excited about.''

Brad whistled and turned to his date. ''I see his signs all over Houston.'' He looked back at Rick. ''I live in Houston now. There was quite a write-up on you in the business section of the *Sunday Chronicle* a few weeks ago.''

Rick's expression darkened. ''I don't really want to make a big deal out of it. It's just what I do for a living.''

He scanned the crowd again.

''Who would have ever thought,'' Brad continued, ''you and Tracy both making it big. Isn't that wild about her being on network television?''

Rick's forehead creased. ''Well, I guess that's what she wants someday.''

Brad shook his head. ''Haven't you heard? She's leaving here to go to an interview. Little Tracy has finally hit the big time.''

Rick's head reeled. He loved Tracy enough to want her to have what she wanted out of life. But, God help him, he hated this.

She was slipping out of his life again, and he couldn't hold her back.

He masked his astonishment, raising one hand to his shirt pocket, where he felt in it the hard circle of gold and diamonds he had brought back from Houston.

There was no need for it now.

''Speaking of Tracy, did you see where she took off to?''

Brad pointed toward the edge of the woods. ''The last time I saw her, she was walking toward the edge of the woods with Shannon's cousin.''

Sudden irrational anger rushed through Rick's veins. He'd spent too many years watching Tracy walk off with Shannon. He wasn't about to have her attention taken by Sam on one of their last nights together.

"Excuse me," he said curtly, marching off toward the woods. As he neared them, he heard Tracy's light laughter drifting out of the darkness.

He followed the sound, stopping dead in his tracks and feeling foolish as he found them sitting on stumps several feet away from each other.

Their conversation had stopped abruptly at his arrival, and both were staring up at him expectantly.

"I was worried about you," he told Tracy limply.

"Sam and I were just talking," she said. "Pull up a stump."

Sam got to his feet. "You can have mine. I feel the need to singe another marshmallow." He took off toward the party.

After he was gone, Rick stood looking down at Tracy. "He didn't have to rush off."

"Can you blame him? You looked like you were about to punch him in the nose."

"You know I hate violence."

"He doesn't know that. What's wrong, Rick? You're not acting like yourself."

"Nothing," he said absently.

Now that they were finally alone, he had little to say to her. She was on the brink of a future she'd always dreamed about. He wouldn't be asking her to marry him.

The faint sound of a ballad came through the woods. He leaned down and grasped her hand.

"Let's dance," he coaxed.

"All right," she agreed, submitting to his strength as he pulled her up. All she'd wanted these past few days was to be in his arms again. But now that he was here, she had a sudden, panicky feeling something was terribly wrong.

He held her close, moving slowly to the faraway music, pressing her head against his chest with one broad palm.

Tracy's doubts began melting away as she gave in to the dark quiet of the woods, the fresh, damp scent of moss and leaves, and the tender way he held her. As she buried her face in the folds of his shirt, his closeness overpowered her senses.

Rick thought of all the things he'd been planning to say. The things he couldn't say now. But was he strong enough to give her up?

"Rick?"

He realized she was calling his name. Still holding her, he looked down.

"The music's ended," she told him.

He smiled. "So it has."

She searched his face. "It's so good to have you

back, Rick. Why didn't you call and tell us you were coming? Why didn't you call?''

''I thought of it a million times.''

She drew away from him. ''Will it be that way again when I leave? I'm not going to hear from you, am I?''

''I didn't say that.''

Her eyes narrowed. ''You've always been better at listening than talking. When you were gone and I didn't hear from you, I didn't know what to think.''

''I guess I'm not good at small talk.''

She drew away from him, walking over to the stump and planting herself on it with her arms crossed. Then she looked up at him anxiously. ''I love you, Rick. Let's not lose each other again.''

He knelt beside her. ''That's the last thing I want. I love you, Trace. Remember that.''

Looping one hand behind her neck, he drew her close and kissed her, a long, leisurely kiss.

Tracy thought her heart would burst. When she remembered this was their last night together here, she nearly cried. She didn't want to argue with him, either. How often in your life do you find that one, perfect love? She wanted to stay with him, wherever he was. Why was he telling her to remember he loved her? She wanted him to tell her again and again.

But what would he think if she told him that?

"Let's not fight tonight," Rick urged. "We have time to work everything out."

She shook her head. "We don't," she countered, her words falling like missiles. "I'm leaving in the morning."

His eyes rounded. "Tomorrow morning?"

She nodded solemnly. "I've got to go to New York. I have an interview with the network. They called while you were gone."

He forced a smile, but she recognized the sadness in it.

"It's your dream. It's coming true," he said with false cheer.

"Maybe I could call them, change the date . . ." she began.

"Don't," he snapped.

She pulled back, staring at him in surprise.

"Don't change it. It might hurt your chances of getting the job."

"Yes, that's what's important, I suppose," she said.

Her sarcasm was lost on Rick. The tightness in his chest nearly caused him physical pain. In the back of his mind, he'd always believed if he was successful, he would be able to have anything he wanted. Now he saw how futile that was. He could buy Tracy anything she wanted, but he could never give her what she wanted most—her own shot at success.

He had to let her go. And he had to let her go without feeling their parting was her fault. He knew how Tracy's mind worked. She was still blaming herself for leaving Shannon.

Shannon, who she knew hadn't really loved her.

He leaned forward and kissed her so thoroughly her senses soared.

She had never loved like this, never would again.

He drew back, smiling down on her and searching her face as though he were trying to imprint it in his memory.

And from his look, Tracy knew her fears were well-founded. She wasn't going to be seeing him once she left. Maybe he'd loved her once. And maybe he loved her a little now. But not enough to make a commitment to their future.

If it was over, there was no point staying out here and tearing her heart apart.

"We'd better go back," she announced abruptly.

His jaw slackened as though she'd offended him. Didn't he know how he was torturing her? she wondered.

"All right," he agreed, although he was reluctant to return to the crowd.

When he helped her up, he felt her stiffen under his touch.

But it was better, he reminded himself, that she be angry with him than with herself. He would not put her in a position where she had to choose between him and her future.

He followed her to the clearing in silence.

Tracy gasped as she stepped out of the woods to find nothing there but a pile of drenched ashes that had been the campfire.

"They've left us behind!" she exclaimed indignantly.

"Seems like your dad would have noticed his own daughter was missing," Rick observed.

Her hands flew to her hips as she assessed the situation.

"I guess we'll just have to walk back," she concluded.

"It's not that far," he ventured.

She shot him a blazing look. How could he tell her he loved her and just leave it at that forever? He hadn't even asked how he could get in touch with her in Dallas.

She marched off across the field without waiting for him.

"Hey, slow down," he called.

Grudgingly, she waited for him to catch up.

"You're the one who's leaving," he reminded her.

"We both knew this would happen," she said. "I just didn't plan on everything that happened in between."

"We'll always be friends," he said.

His words pierced her like arrows. So that was what it all came back to. Tracy felt tears well in the corners of her eyes. Friends just wasn't enough anymore. She never should have let this happen. Yet how could she have stopped it?

"Remember when we were climbing that steep incline by the creek and you slipped?" he asked.

She did remember. A wistful smile crossed her expression. "It was muddy that day, and you caught me halfway down. Probably saved me from breaking my neck."

She remembered that gray, overcast day well. Trembling and heart hammering, she'd found herself suddenly tumbling into Rick's strong arms, and she'd clung to him for dear life while he talked her the rest of the way down the slope.

Wasn't that the first inkling she'd had that her feelings for Rick went beyond friendship? But she'd shrugged it off later, because her teenage heart focused on Shannon.

She felt her resolve crumbling. If she had to leave Rick behind, she didn't want to leave him in anger.

"Will you come and see me?" She hated having to ask.

"Try to keep me away," Rick answered, surprising her.

Her spirits lifted a little, but she wondered, too, whether she'd forced him into a lie. Would they have the time her mother said they needed?

Rick caught hold of her hand, easing some of her doubts.

As they reached the porch, Tracy moved to go inside, but Rick stopped her.

"Don't go in just yet," he asked.

"All right," she agreed, easing onto the step beside him.

She gazed at the quiet street, the star-studded sky overhead. A soft breeze ruffled the branches on the trees. Cherry Cove was asleep.

She sighed deeply. "I'd forgotten what it was like to be in a place this quiet."

"Me, too."

For a few moments they sat in silence, reflecting on the old times and the new.

"What time are you leaving in the morning?" he asked.

"Early. My flight leaves Houston at ten."

"I can drive you to the airport."

She shrugged. "My car's a rental. I've got to turn it in."

"I'll have someone pick it up for you."

"I couldn't let you put anyone to that much trouble."

He reached in his pocket, producing the slim gold band, and caught her hand in his.

"I want you to have this," he said, slipping the ring on her finger.

Tracy incredulously gaped at the gold and diamonds glittering beneath the porchlight.

"I can't keep this," she protested, her eyes lighting on his face.

"Please take it, Tracy."

But she twisted it off her finger and placed it in his palm. "It's far too expensive," she said, unaware she was shaking.

It was obviously an engagement ring. But why was he giving it to her? Why did he have it? Had he planned to ask her to marry him and changed his mind? Why?

Rick looked down at the sparkler in his hand. He didn't understand why she refused it, but he suspected she was afraid he would ask for a commitment from her with it.

Silently he slipped it back into his pocket.

"I just wanted you to remember what these last few days have meant to me," he said.

Her eyes rolled. "Oh, God, Rick. Do you think I could ever forget these past few days?"

He pressed close and gave her a kiss that made her wish she were never leaving.

"Knock 'em dead in New York, Hotshot," he whispered. "Can we have breakfast together before you leave?"

"Sure. Meet me on the back porch at seven. Will you be going back to Houston soon?"

"Tomorrow, I expect. There's no reason to stay

now that . . . now that Sam's come to take care of the store."

"It's getting late. I think we both need some sleep."

He pressed something into her hand as she got up. She looked down, dumbfounded to see his business card in her hand.

"Call if you need me," he said.

She nodded dully. "Thanks." She knew she wouldn't call. Long ago he had always been there to catch her when her heart was in pieces. Now he couldn't offer her any comfort because he was the one breaking it.

"Good night, Rick," she said.

"Good night, Trace."

Rick woke to the sound of birds singing outside. Sleepily, he peered at the alarm clock and saw it was ten to seven.

Quickly, he jumped out of bed, dressing and shaving in record time.

He had been wrong last night, he decided. Whether or not they would be together was as much Tracy's decision as his. Before she left, he had to tell her he wanted her as his wife, he wanted a family. And somehow they could find a way to have that together and their other lives, too.

That settled in his mind, he raced downstairs,

zipping past a bemused Mrs. Madison in the kitchen to the back porch.

Disappointment cut through him when he saw Tracy wasn't there yet.

He sat down on the railing to wait, a knot twisting in his stomach as he looked at his watch and discovered it was five after. It wasn't like her to be late. Well, she had to pack. Maybe she was just running behind.

The back door opened, and he looked up, thinking it was her. But Mrs. Madison came through the door instead. She handed him a mug of coffee.

"She's gone, isn't she?" he asked.

Alice nodded. "She said to tell you she was sorry but she couldn't go through saying good-bye again."

Rick kicked the porch railing. "I've lost her again," he said.

"You let her go. No one who loved her could have done less."

"I'm not so sure. I didn't ask her what she wanted."

"We all know what she wants," Alice reminded him.

Rick looked up at Tracy's mother, and suddenly he saw that much of what Tracy believed she wanted was what her mother wanted for her. He couldn't blame Alice. She had only one child. Naturally she wanted what she believed was best for her.

But hadn't Alice planted a lot of ideas in Tracy's

head? Even in the old days, Alice was always commenting on how good Tracy looked with Shannon, how Tracy was meant for bigger things than Cherry Cove had to offer.

All these years she'd been subtly steering Tracy away from Rick, even though she could see they were in love, something her daughter herself couldn't see.

"You don't want Tracy to get married, do you?" he blurted.

A look of astonishment crossed Alice's face. "Someday, of course. I want her to be happy." Her expression hardened. "But I was always afraid she would marry one of you local boys before she reached her potential."

Rick looked at Alice as though he were seeing her for the first time. "So you encouraged her to date Shannon because you could see he wasn't the marrying kind."

"Tracy makes her own decisions."

"But you were always there, in the background. She confided in you. We all did."

"I was relieved when your family moved away," she admitted.

"I wondered why Tracy never answered any of my letters."

"She never got them," Alice admitted. "You were the one that always worried me."

"How could you?"

"I thought things might be different when you got back. Honestly, Rick, I tried to make up for it. I was on your side. But then the call came from the network."

"What did you say to her this morning?"

"Nothing. I—"

"Did you suggest she leave without seeing me?"

"She was already talking about giving up her career. I could see how distraught she was."

Rick rose, standing tall. "Alice, I love your daughter. And if she'll have me, I intend to marry her. She'll never be happy unless she can decide for herself what she wants."

The tears in Alice's eyes laced his anger with sympathy.

"Don't tell her," she pleaded.

He shook his head. "Tracy would never believe it if I did. That's something you'll have to work out with her."

He walked past her toward the door. "I'll get my things. I'm going back to Houston. I'll write you a check for the bill."

Midway through the screen door, he paused. "What hurts the most is that all these years I thought you were my friend."

Alice turned away and gazed off into the woods.

She had never meant to deprive her daughter of the happiness she deserved. But now she wondered whether that wasn't exactly what she had accomplished.

Chapter Nine

Tracy glanced down at the gold-embossed business card in her hand, then up at the glass skyscraper looming before her. Yes, it was the address Rick had given her.

She had expected something more modest, a wooden shack with piles of receipts and tools lying all over the place. Sawdust on the floor.

With a shrug, she proceeded through the revolving door, the doorman's curious stare making her suddenly a little self-conscious about her casual jeans and shirt. Coming here had been a sudden decision.

"Excuse me, ma'am."

She turned to see the doorman racing after her. She forced a wide smile, masking her apprehension. After coming all this way, was she about to be turned back by the doorman? She couldn't let that happen. Rick was up there somewhere, and she had to see him.

The past few days were a blur. She'd been to New York, then to Dallas. All the while, she'd felt cold and empty.

Even her own apartment didn't feel like home anymore. Then came that strange phone call from her mother. She'd sounded like she was crying and mumbling about Rick and letters and how she was sorry. Tracy still didn't understand, but she was beginning to.

Her mother, she realized, had been trying to keep Rick from interfering with her career. Why hadn't she seen it? Why had she overlooked such obvious hints?

And what had inspired that phone call?

Her head was spinning. Now she was trying to sort out how much in her life was her own doing and how much was her mother's.

She had to see Rick.

Now, looking up at the doorman, who was younger than she'd first thought, she blinked innocently, all the while hating herself for putting on such a charade.

"Yes?" she asked, as though she hadn't a clue as to what he might want.

"Can I help you find someone?" he asked.

"I'm on my way up to Evans Construction. I'm a friend of Mr. Evans."

He nodded evenly, convincing her he didn't believe her. She wished she had changed clothes. If she were wearing a dress or a suit, he wouldn't have given her a second glance.

"Look," she said as he made no move to let her past him into the elevator. "Don't you recognize me? I'm Tracy Madison. My show's on cable."

Apparently he was the one individual in Texas who didn't know who she was. Just her luck.

He shook his head, now apparently believing she was a lunatic.

"I've never heard of you," he said in a thick drawl.

But a white-haired man in a brown suit and a Stetson overheard them as he was passing by. He stopped, beaming at Tracy.

"Let her go, Albert. She is Tracy Madison."

Tracy breathed a sigh of relief as Albert, his eyes still suspiciously narrowed on her, moved aside.

She looked up at the stranger. "Thank you," she said, following him onto the elevator.

"You can't blame Albert. He does a good job."

"I can see that," she admitted.

"But I would appreciate an autograph for my daughter, if you don't mind."

"Sure," Tracy replied, fishing in her purse for a

pen. She was so grateful, she could have kissed the old man.

She said good-bye to him on the fourth floor, as he got off with the autograph in hand.

Strange, she thought as the elevator zipped up to the thirtieth floor, leaving her stomach behind, she'd already decided before her mother's phone call that she would come here to see Rick. If nothing else, she had to know why he'd bought that ring. If he was going to propose, why had he changed his mind?

She got off the elevator, following the signs to Evans Construction. As she stepped inside the office, she drew in a deep breath, inspecting the Oriental rugs on the polished floors, crystal lamps on the mahogany tables, plush upholstered chairs.

A secretary sat before a desk, and Rick's voice drifted through an intercom. "Try that Dallas number again, Loretta, please."

The woman in the beige linen suit, with red hair swept high up on her head, looked up at Tracy as though she were about to ask her to leave. Suddenly she broke into a smile.

"I don't think I'll need to," she replied through the box, then pushed a button on the phone.

"Go right in, Miss Madison. Please go right in."

Tracy smiled appreciatively, then approached the door to the inner office. But before she could reach it, it opened.

She nearly didn't recognize Rick in his blue suit and striped tie.

"What do you mean you won't have to—" he demanded, breaking his words off in mid-sentence as he spotted Tracy.

"Rick?" she asked in astonishment.

"Tracy?"

Muttering a hasty apology to his secretary, he pulled Tracy inside and quickly closed the door. Without waiting for explanations, he wound his arms around her and kissed her deeply. Her sneakered feet threatened to leave the floor.

"I can't believe you're here," he said finally.

"You're not angry with me?" she asked.

"For leaving without saying good-bye? Yes, of course I am. But I'm sure you had your reasons."

"They didn't seem to hold much credence by the time I was halfway to the airport."

"So you came all this way to say good-bye?"

"No. I just came to get a few things straight."

She folded her arms and strolled over to the window, looking down on the streets of downtown Houston that from here resembled a toy race track. Standing so close to Rick, still tingling from his powerful kiss, it was impossible to think straight.

She looked around. "Rick, what is all this? You said you had a little company."

"Well, it started out that way."

"Why didn't you tell me? I'm so proud of you."

"Would it have made any difference?"

"In how I feel about you? No, nothing would."

"Then there wasn't any point."

"But your house is so . . . so . . ."

"Average?"

"Yes!"

"I've lived there for a long time. I didn't want to move."

She rolled her eyes in exasperation, walking over to the desk and dropping down in his cushioned leather chair.

"Do you always have to be so silent, so stoic?"

"What do you mean?"

"How could you just sit back all those years and not tell me how you really felt?"

A vein throbbed in his neck. "You know the answer to that."

"No. I don't think I do. I think if I'd had reason to stop and think about it, I would have realized then it was you I was in love with all along."

"There's no point in going back over the past, Tracy."

"You were trying to call me."

"Because there was something I forgot to say to you."

"What was that?"

He walked over to the desk, turning the swivel chair to the side and planting one hand on each armrest. He leaned down close.

"I wanted to ask you to marry me."

Tracy blinked incredulously.

"Why didn't you?"

"Because I didn't want to make you choose between me and your job."

"Why can't you let me decide what's best for me? You're as bad as my mother . . ."

She saw his face go pale. "You know what she's been doing, don't you? Trying to keep us apart to ensure I went to New York."

He nodded. "How do you know?"

"I was beginning to suspect it as I was driving to the airport. That morning what she said made sense—that saying good-bye might be too hard for both of us. Later I wondered if she was afraid it would be so difficult that we wouldn't go through with it. Then she called when I got back to Dallas and admitted what she'd been doing all these years. Did you write me some letters after you moved away?"

"Yes."

"Why didn't you mention them?"

"So many years had passed. I didn't think it made any difference. Besides, I thought you had gotten them and just not answered."

"I would have answered them. I missed you a lot once you left. I can't believe my own mother would do this to me. She used to always warn me not to get too serious about the boys in Cherry Cove. I thought it was just talk, you know. Especially because she never minded my going out with Shannon. I never thought she would do anything like this. It was me and you she was worried about."

"She was just overprotective, Tracy. I don't think she meant to manipulate you as much as she actually did."

"Don't defend her. I don't know if I can ever face her again."

"Everyone makes mistakes."

She looked up at him with wide eyes. "Yes, everyone does."

"How was your interview?"

"I've got the job."

He kissed her lightly, leaving her wanting more. "Way to go, Hotshot. This calls for a celebration."

She glanced down at her jeans. "I'm hardly dressed to be seen in public with you."

He looked down at his own clothes. "I had a meeting this afternoon," he explained. "I know a place where it won't matter."

She smiled. "Let's go. Oh, can you leave?"

"Of course I can leave. I'm the boss."

"Did you bring a car?" he asked as they headed for the elevator.

"No. I took the bus."

"I still can't believe you came all this way."

"I owed it to you after the way I left."

Downstairs, Tracy delighted in Albert's astonished expression as she and Rick stepped off the elevator.

"Just a minute," she told Rick.

She walked over to Albert and stuffed a bill in his hand. "You're doing a great job," she told him, then walked back to rejoin Rick.

"What was that all about?" Rick asked.

On the way to the parking garage where he kept his car, she told him. Rick howled with laughter.

"I feel pretty safe now, knowing he's doing his job," he said. "Maybe it's not so different from what your mother was doing."

"I don't want to discuss that anymore. I'm furious with her."

Rick let the subject drop.

He stopped at a restaurant a few miles away and ordered a takeout meal, then continued on to the tree-lined neighborhood she recognized as his.

"Cecil's been asking about you," he said.

"I'll bet."

Cecil did come bounding out the door when Rick opened it, wagging his tail and jumping on her legs.

Tracy reached down and rubbed the dog's head.

After they were inside, Rick put him in the yard. Tracy helped him set the table, complete with candlesticks and tapers. Rick lit the candles and spread out the cartons of food. There was lemon chicken, sauteed shrimp, coleslaw, potato salad, rolls.

"I think there's more than the two of us can eat," she observed.

"We'll just have to do our best."

She couldn't remember a meal having tasted better. When they were finished, she started picking up the dishes, but he stopped her.

"I'll get that later," he assured her.

He gestured for her to follow him into the living room.

She did.

He put a CD on the stereo and drew her into his arms. "Dinner, dancing, candlelight. I guess everything is perfect now."

She looked up at him. "You're driving me mad," she said.

He cast her an innocent glance.

"You said," she continued, "that you had forgotten to ask me to marry you. Are you asking or what?"

Rick laughed deeply. "Yes, I'm asking." His expression grew serious as his eyes probed hers. "Will you be my wife, Tracy? I don't know how we'll manage it, but I know we can somehow. I know it won't be easy at first, but I have an idea."

Tracy looked into the eyes of the man who had for so long been her best friend and was now her love as well. She had never trusted more completely. If Rick believed their long-distance relationship would work, she believed it, too. A brand-new love song played in her heart.

"Yes. I want us to be together. Even if it's not easy."

"Not much ever has been for us," he said, cupping her chin and kissing her as though she were a rare treasure he'd discovered. "But I promise you things will get better. There's just one thing we have to do first."

"What's that?" she asked, savoring his kiss.

"We need to go see your mother."

Her expression dulled. Then she slowly raised her eyes to meet his, and she knew he was right.

"Let's go," she agreed.

EPILOGUE

In the Texas twilight, Tracy pulled up in front of the sprawling ranch outside Houston, pleased to see Rick's pickup in the drive. This had been a long day of filming, and then her doctor's appointment, but there was always Rick to come home to.

She stood for a moment, studying the colors of the sky as the sun set and inhaling country air that was heavy with rain.

She thought briefly of Shannon, as she sometimes did, her heart filling with sadness but no regret. Then she turned her thoughts to the new life inside her.

Cecil bounded out to greet her. She patted him, then proceeded toward the stables. She walked straight there, pulling off her cumbersome high heels midstep and carrying them. Fashion was fine for the city, but impractical out here.

Rick was inside, pitching hay. Its sweet smell reminded her of their kisses in the barn one summer night.

For a long moment, she watched him work, enjoying his determined, efficient movement.

"Hi," he said, his face lighting up when he saw her.

"Hi, yourself."

"How was your day?" he asked.

"Long, but good. Yours?" She set her shoes down and took off her cotton blazer.

"Pretty good. You've got a real funny look on your face."

"Mom called and said she and Dad will be up this weekend."

"That doesn't bother you?"

She tossed her headful of curls. "You know how difficult it's been working things out with Mom, but I think we're making progress. She and I are both trying."

Rick gave her one of his rare grins. "Something tells me you have more on your mind than that then. Come on, what is it?"

She nodded, standing on tiptoe to give him an impulsive kiss.

"Come on, Hotshot. Out with it."

"Well, you know, Rick, I might have gotten on

network television on my own, but without your business savvy, I never would have been able to start my own production company and come back to Houston.''

''I had selfish motives,'' he pointed out. ''I was tired of having my wife in New York more than with me.''

''Well, I thought it was time I pitched in and did something for the family.''

''Such as?'' His interest keened, he set the pitchfork down.

''Such as having a baby,'' she blurted.

Rick let out a whoop, scooping her up in both arms. ''Oh, sweetheart,'' he told her between kisses. ''And I'm still just getting used to the fact that we're really together.''

''You'll have lots of time for that,'' she reminded him. ''The rest of our lives.''

Tracy hugged his neck as he carried her toward the house. She'd never dreamed it was possible to love this much. She held on tight, not because she was afraid he'd drop her, but because she never wanted to lose her grip on what was best in her life.

Rick had always been there for her, and she would always be there for him. A glorious love song echoed in her heart.